THE BUTCHER'S SON

THE
BUTCHER'S
SON

gay mystery novel by

DORIEN GREY

E-Book Division of
GLB Publishers

San Francisco

Published in the United States by
GLB Publishers
P.O. Box 78212, San Francisco, CA 94107 USA

Cover by GLB Publishers

ISBN 1-879194-86-4

Library of Congress Card Number:

2001086705

2001

To all those
who led the way

CHAPTER 1

As hard as it is for me to remember, sometimes, I haven't always been a private investigator. None of us starts life doing what we end up doing, of course, but how we get where we are instead of someplace else is often pretty fascinating to contemplate. Now, in my case…

* * *

Did you ever have one of those years? You know: you start New Years' day with a hangover and everything just goes downhill from there? Well, it was one of those years. I was stuck in a job I hated and Chris, my lover of five years, was getting the seven year itch two years early. We'd been together ever since shortly after we got out of college, and each of us was the other's first real relationship, so I guess you couldn't really blame him. That, plus the fact that we lived in a gay ghetto, so the candy store syndrome made it easy enough to stray for anyone so inclined, and Chris became increasingly inclined.

But we were hanging in there, putting on the good old "perfect couple" routine whenever anyone else was around and working on matching ulcers when they weren't. I was up to two-and-a-half packs of cigarettes a day and rising; Chris was devoting considerable time to adding to his swizzle-stick collection. All in all, a real fun time.

Chris was always a lot more into bars than I was, so it wasn't unusual for him to go out by himself, though I noted that lately he'd been going out a lot more than normal. We did hold to our Saturday-night-out-to-dinner tradition though, after which we'd stop in at the Ebony Room, a nice little neighborhood bar close to home, for a nightcap. This particular night, however, Chris suggested we go to a new bar he'd found, Bacchus' Lair, which he said had a great drag show. I should have put "great" in quotes, since I was never much for drag, but Chris got a kick out of it, so we went.

I should also point out that this was after Stonewall, but not all that much, and the community hadn't completely gotten its act together in most cities. Blatant homophobia was the attitude of choice for most police forces, and ours was particularly noted for its less-than-tolerant methods. It was also a solid source of income for the city—bust a gay bar, haul in 30 or 40 gays too scared or too poor to fight it, charge them with "lewd and lascivious conduct," drop the charges down to "disturbing the peace" and slap a $350 fine for a "no contest" plea. The city was happy; the police were happy; the lawyers were happy. The gays weren't happy, but who cared?

Bacchus' Lair was located in a former loft upstairs over a discount furniture store on the edge of skid row. A lot of gay bars were in this area, probably partly because of the lower rents, and the smaller likelihood that neighbors would complain about the clientele. Bacchus' Lair was decorated in Early Flamboyant—tables the size of dinner plates, purple tablecloths, purple carpet, purple stage curtains, wall fixtures with dangly globs of plastic that I suppose the management thought looked like grapes. Wall niches with little gold cherubs shouldering platters of plastic grapes. Oh, and a cover charge. And a two-watered-down-drink minimum. But you got to keep the little purple umbrellas that came with them.

There were a few people there we knew—I should say a few people I knew—Chris seemed to know a lot more. We were shown to a table—I asked for one by an exit—by a lesbian in full male drag—a nice touch of equality, I thought. We ordered our drinks just as the canned music announcing the start of the show blared out across the room, making conversation impossible. The room lights dimmed, the curtains opened (revealing a stage about three feet deep), and the show began.

If you've seen one drag show, you saw this one. Not too bad, really; the usual standard numbers by the usual standard drag queens. Only one—a huge black drag named, if you could believe the M.C., Tondelaya O'Tool—did her own material and was really talented.

Intermission arrived with the inevitable, and inevitably "cute", announcement by the M.C. that "We'll be right back after a wee-wee break." The curtains closed, the lights came back up, and the waiters rushed throughout the room restocking the what-passed-for-liquor. Also as usual, some of the entertainers came down to mix with the customers.

"Well," Chris said, "what did you think? Great, huh?"

I nodded. "Great."

"Yeah," Chris said, "but wait until the second half— that's when Judy comes on. She's fantastic."

I was willing to take his word for it. "I'm surprised how crowded it is," I said.

"Do I detect a note of the famous Dick Hardesty paranoia?" Chris asked. "I notice you insisted on sitting near an exit again."

"You didn't think it was paranoia when I yanked your ass out of the Bull Pen the night the cops raided it," I said. "If we hadn't been near an exit, we'd have been hauled in like everybody else."

"Well, you don't have to worry here," Chris said, leaning back in his chair. "They've never had a raid."

"And how long have they been open?" I asked.

Chris shrugged. "I dunno. Two months, maybe."

"That long, huh? Maybe they should hang up a sign: 'A fine tradition of excellence since June.'"

Chris grinned and shook his head. "You're crazy, Hardesty."

Tondelaya O'Tool had come down from the stage and moved through the room like a fully laden oil tanker in heavy seas, bestowing forehead kisses, Queen of England waves, and assorted quips to the customers. Spotting Chris, she plowed her way to our table.

"How ya doin', Chris darlin'?" she asked Chris, her eyes deliberately moving back and forth between Chris and me, one eyebrow raised.

"Great, Teddy," Chris said. "Great show tonight."

Tondelaya-nee-Teddy put one hand on her more than ample hip and made a "get away with you, now" gesture with the other, a la Pearl Bailey.

"Why thank you, darlin'," she said. Then, looking at me, she gave a slow, exaggerated tongue-extended lip-lick and said "And who's this good-lookin' hunk o' man?"

Chris grinned. "This is my other half, Dick Hardesty."

Tondelaya/Teddy extended a hand. "I'll just bet he is," she said as I took it—and was surprised by an unexpectedly strong grip. "My, you two make a handsome couple, don't you, now?"

"We try," I said.

"Can we buy you a drink?" Chris asked.

"I really shouldn't," she said while in one continuous movement sweeping a chair from a nearby table and motioning the waiter. "But I am parched and I do have a minute or two before I have to get back. Scotch rocks, double," she said to the waiter who disappeared as quickly as he'd come.

"So how do you like working here?" I asked for want of anything better to say.

"Oh, I love it, honey. *Love* it. It's a lot better than the Galaxy, that's for sure."

"Didn't that burn down a month or so ago?" I asked.

Tondelaya/Teddy reached out and tapped my arm. "That it did, chile, that it did. That's when I came over here. I was lucky, really. There's gettin' to be fewer an' fewer drag clubs around what with the raids an' the fires an' all. A lot of my friends are just plain out of work."

"So what time is Judy coming on?" Chris asked, demonstrating his usual short attention span.

Tondelaya/Teddy took the drink the waiter brought, downed it in one gulp, and shrugged. "Same as every night. You know she's always the last act. Save the best for last, that's her motto." Suddenly she put her hand to her mouth and lowered her voice. "I didn't say that," she said between her fingers. "You never heard me say that, okay?"

"Okay," Chris and I said in unison, exchanging a puzzled glance.

"Good." Tondelaya/Teddy pushed herself back from the table, nearly knocking our drinks on the floor in the process, and got up. "I gotta go get changed. You liked the first act, honeys, just wait 'til you see the second." With a broad stage grin, she moved off toward the dressing room.

"What was that last part all about?" I asked Chris.

He shrugged. "I have no idea."

The waiter arrived unbidden, bringing two more drinks (unordered) just as the house lights dimmed and the second act began. It was more of the same, except for Tondelaya/ Teddy, who did a really good down-and-dirty blues number I'd always associated with one of my favorite old army cadences:

"I'm not the butcher, I'm the butcher's son;
But I'll give you meat until the butcher comes."

She was followed by a marginally-passable Diana Ross imitator, a slightly better Barbara Streisand imitator, and somebody who apparently thought—wrongly—he/she was Sophie Tucker.

"Judy's next," Chris leaned over to me and whispered.

The curtains closed, and the room went completely dark until a small spotlight came on, the music started, and a voice said: "Ladies and gentlemen, Miss Judy Garland!" The curtains opened to…Judy Garland. Quite a bit taller and not as frail, but Judy Garland nonetheless. I realized it wasn't even the face; it was the posture, the movements, the little gestures. Perfect. Even before she opened her mouth, I was impressed. This guy was good.

The song was "The Man That Got Away" and instead of just lip-synching, she sang with the record, and it was as if Judy Garland were singing a duet with herself. Chris nudged me and gave me his "I told you so" nod, and I just nodded back.

The end of the record was greeted by tremendous applause, in which I joined wholeheartedly. Judy took a bow, then went immediately into "The Trolley Song," followed by "You Made Me Love You." When she finished, the crowd was on its feet—Chris and I included. The curtains started to close, but the crowd wouldn't have it and she waved them back open, sat on the edge of the stage, and sang, of course, "Over the Rainbow." Even I had a lump in my throat.

When she finished the song, the room went black again and when the lights came back on, she was gone. The other entertainers came out for their curtain calls but, despite chants of "Ju-dy ... Ju-dy" she did not come out, and at last the applause died away and the show was over.

We finished our drinks, paid the bill, and got up to leave.

"I've got to hand it to you, Chris," I said. "That really was great."

Chris put his arm around my shoulder. "After five years you doubted me?" he asked.

*　*　*

I've already mentioned that I hated my job. I'd had several since I left college and didn't feel really comfortable with any of them, but as I've always said, it isn't the principle of the thing, it's the money. At the moment, I was being rather embarrassingly overpaid by a small public relations firm, Carlton Carlson & Associates. The reason for the high salary was that CC&A was run by the rear end of a horse with a monumental ego, and the only way he could keep help was by paying them so much they couldn't afford to go elsewhere. He had, thanks to his rich wife's family connections, passably juggled the careers of one or two fairly well-known clients over the years and had volunteered his—that is to say, his staff's—services in the promotion and setup of a press conference for the Chief of Police's contemplated assault on the governor's seat. His magnanimous gesture was hardly altruistic, since C.C. viewed it as his key to taking over the chief's entire public relations campaign.

The task wouldn't be an easy one, as anyone with his head

a little less far up his behind than my boss would readily have recognized. The chief's political beliefs fell considerably to the right of Atilla the Hun, and he ran his department like Vlad the Impaler. Need I add that he loathed homosexuals? His tact, diplomacy, and delicate handling of any problem involving the gay community had, among some gays, earned him the nickname "The Butcher." But his methods, however reprehensible, had kept the local crime rate in check and he had, until now, kept an extremely low personal profile.

If the chief managed to win the primaries—his opponent was one Marlen Evans, a moderately popular but lackluster state senator—he would be pretty much a shoo-in, since the incumbent governor's wildly liberal policies had alienated the most powerful lobbying groups in the state.

The first step in humanizing the inhuman, my boss decided, was to play up the Chief's warm and loving family life, and guess who got stuck with gathering homey bits about this little nuclear holocaust? Yep, yours truly. The fact that up until now very few people had any idea, or the slightest interest, that the Chief had a license to breed, let alone that he had exercised it five times, left me a pretty open field.

We started by building a rather anemic file of newspaper photos and articles. Of course, the chief's wife was always on hand at functions that required the presence of a spouse, but she generally blended so well with the wallpaper she was almost impossible to pick out if there were more than three people in the picture. Of the children, there was almost nothing known except that the eldest son was a minister and the chief had recently become a grandfather.

It was thereby decreed that I, together with a free-lance writer noted for never having met a subject she didn't like and a photographer selected for his Vaseline-lensed portrait work—both hand picked by C.C. himself, would be sent out to meet with the entire family with the object of getting a feature story into the Sunday supplement of the city's leading newspaper. My sole purpose for being there was a bit vague, other than to ride herd on the writer and photographer, and to steer them clear of the unlikely possibility that they might somehow touch on anything that could smack of controversy. I viewed the entire project with the same enthusiasm as I'd anticipate a root canal, but I had little choice

*   *   *

The interview was set for a Saturday afternoon—my boss not believing in the sanctity of weekends where his employees were involved. We arrived at the chief's Hollywood-back-lot, two-story neo-Georgian home at exactly the appointed hour, and were met at the door by Kathleen Rourke, the chief's wife, looking like a cross between June Cleaver and Donna Reed. She ushered us into the living room, which appeared to have been set up for the photographers from House Beautiful, and Chief Rourke himself, obviously painfully uncomfortable out of his uniform, removed the unlit pipe from his mouth, set it in the chair side ashtray, and rose from a wing-back chair near the fireplace to greet us.

The cursory introductions over, to the obvious relief of both Chief Rourke and me, we were told the rest of the family was gathered on the poolside patio, and followed Mrs. Rourke outside through a set of curtained French doors. Standing around a picnic table at the far end of the pool like deer caught in the headlights was the rest of the Rourke clan.

Chief Rourke, who had followed us outside lest, I suspected, one of us unattended might make a grab for the family silver, made the introductions, clockwise around the table: Tammy, aged 15; Colleen, age 17; Mary, 13; Robert (Robby), 14; and Kevin, the minister, age not given but probably 25, who was accompanied by his lovely wife Sue-Lynn, and their infant son, Sean.

The children, except for Kevin, who had obviously inherited all the good looks, all took after their mother—that is to say, were nondescript to the point that any one of them would be hard to pick out of a police lineup.

I suggested we first get the photos out of the way, and Ted, the photographer, proceeded to take up the next half hour orchestrating various shots of the family around the picnic table, by the barbecue, in the living room, around the kitchen table, etc. It may have just been my imagination, but it seemed like every time I looked at Kevin, he was looking at me But whenever our eyes met, he'd hurriedly look away.

Actually, Ted need have taken only one photo of the chief, since his expression—the proud family man—never changed except for one moment when the baby, who had been handed him reluctantly only after Ted's repeated suggestion, developed a slow leak in the diaper department.

While all this was going on, the writer, in obvious awe of actually being in the presence of someone so prominent as the chief, tried getting responses to a set of routine questions. At one point, after the majority of photos had been taken and the chief and Mrs. Rourke were huddled at one end of the living room with the writer, I wandered over to the mantle to look at a set of family photos. There were individual shots of all the kids, plus Kevin and Sue-Lynn's wedding photo, plus a photo of baby Sean. But one which caught my eye was an older family shot, taken in front of the house apparently when Mary, the youngest child, was a baby. The interesting thing about the picture was that it contained two Kevins.

Kevin, who had been off somewhere with Sue-Lynn changing the baby and had just reentered the living room, apparently noticed me looking at the photo and hurried over. I got the distinct feeling that I'd been caught at something.

"I was just looking at your photos," I said, rather lamely.

"Yes," Kevin said—the first time since we'd arrived that he'd spoken directly to me. "My mother and father are typical proud parents, I guess."

Never having been noted for excessive tact when my curiosity was aroused, I couldn't resist remarking on the photo.

"I hope I'm not touching a sensitive area," I said, "but I

notice in this one photo there seem to be two of you. I didn't know you had an identical twin."

"Patrick," he said.

Suddenly we were both aware that the chief had gotten up from the sofa, crossed the room, and was, like a thundercloud at a picnic, hovering just behind us.

"Sue-Lynn needs you, Kevin," he said, though how he might have come by that information was totally beyond me, since he'd been seated at the other end of the room for the past ten minutes. Kevin turned without a word and left the room the way he'd come in, leaving me standing there with the chief. The beaming family man facade was gone. His eyes were cold, black holes and his voice sent a chill down my spine.

"Patrick's dead," he said.

CHAPTER 2

By the time I got back home from the meeting with the chief's little brood, the first thing I wanted was a long, hot shower, followed by a drink. Chris wasn't home when I arrived, but was in the kitchen unpacking a sack of groceries when I came in from the bedroom to fix my drink.

"Do I need to ask how it went?" Chris asked, opening the refrigerator to hand me an ice cube tray and to put away a package of chicken.

"Imagine Adolph and Eva with kids," I replied, looking for an ashtray and, as usual, not finding one. I turned on the tap just enough to put out my cigarette, tossed it in the garbage, and reached for the cupboard where we kept the liquor. "You want one?" I asked, taking a glass from the shelf.

Chris shook his head. "I'll wait," he said, folding the bag carefully and putting it in the broom closet with about 10,000 other bags. He then opened another drawer, rummaged around a moment, and handed me a small glass ashtray. "Oh," he said, "do you remember those fire trucks that woke us up last night? It was the Ebony Room."

"Oh, no. How bad?" I asked, pouring bourbon into my glass.

"Gutted," Chris said. "Somebody tossed a fire bomb in through the bathroom window, I hear. It was after closing, thank God, so nobody was hurt."

"Somebody there is that does not like gay bars," I said, paraphrasing Robert Frost. "This makes...what...six in two months?" I set my drink on the counter and reached into my shirt pocket for another cigarette.

"At least," Chris said as he put away the last of the groceries.

"Did you talk to Bob?" I asked, walking into the living room and sitting in my favorite chair. Bob Allen was the owner of the

Ebony Room and lived in our building with his lover, Ramón, a really cute Puerto Rican about 15 years Bob's junior. We weren't exactly friends, but we were, as Chris would say, close acquaintances.

"No," Chris said, following me into the living room. He took my glass and took a sip of my drink, then shuddered dramatically. "*Smooooth*," he said, handing the glass back to me and then plopping himself down on the sofa. "Tony called right after you left this morning to tell me about it, and I tried calling Bob right after that, but nobody was home."

I shook my head. "I'm really sorry about that," I said. "We'll just have to find another place to hang out."

"Speaking of which," Chris said, "are you up to dinner out tonight, or do you just want to drink yourself into a stupor here?"

I carefully put my cigarette in the ashtray and gave Chris the finger. "One drink does not a stupor make," I said, "and, yes, I'm up to going out. God knows I deserve it after today."

"Good," Chris said, getting up from the sofa and moving down the hall to the bedroom. "I'm going to hit the shower and start getting ready."

*   *   *

A thunderstorm had broken by the time we reached Rasputin's, a slightly overpriced but very trendy and therefore popular gay restaurant/bar close to downtown. I wasn't as much into either trendy or popular as Chris was, but I didn't feel like making an issue of it. I'd discovered when we were about halfway there that I may well have deserved a night on the town, but I didn't really feel much like it.

We were having a drink at the bar while waiting for our table when someone came up behind us and grabbed us both around the shoulders. A deep voice said "Well, honey lambs, I do declare you make a gorgeous couple." We turned in unison to face a very large black man with exaggeratedly pursed lips, whose eyes darted back and forth between us without moving his head. It wasn't until he broke into a wide grin that I recognized Tondelaya O'Tool in his Teddy persona.

We exchanged greetings, and his large hands rested easily on our shoulders. "So what are you two lovelies doing out on a night like this?" Tondelaya/Teddy asked.

"Our Saturday night ritual," Chris said. "Old habits are hard to break, even in bad weather."

"You having dinner?" T/T asked.

"If we ever get a table," I said.

"Well, stay away from the lamb chops; they're deadly," T/T advised.

"Can we buy you a drink?" Chris asked.

T/T pulled both of us to him. "Oh, thank you, honeys, but I've got to get to the club. Show time in about an hour. Are you coming over?"

Chris looked at me, and I shook my head. "Not tonight, I'm afraid," Chris said. "The master here has a headache."

"We'll try for next Saturday," I said.

T/T slapped us both on the back. "Well, you just better. I'll be looking for you, hear?"

*   *   *

Some people are lucky enough to have jobs in which each day is a joyful blur. Chris' job was like that: he was head window designer for Marston's, the most prestigious (and expensive) department store in the city, and he already had a solid reputation in the industry. He couldn't wait to get to work every day. My work days were more like psychedelic smudges—they were just one long blur when viewed in retrospect, but were endless when viewed from each morning looking toward evening.

The writer, who had done other assignments for my boss, wisely sent her cloyingly adulatory piece on the Clan Rourke in on Tuesday morning by messenger. The boss demanded to see it immediately, then scornfully proclaiming her to be "a no-talent hack" (I resisted pointing out that he was the one who had hired her) insisted that I personally make several totally unnecessary additions and changes.

The photographer, not as shrewd as the writer, brought his contact sheets into the office himself on Wednesday afternoon. I thought they were quite good, considering what he had to work with, but the boss viewed them with his usual total contempt, making it clear that his own four year old son could have done an infinitely superior job with an old Polaroid and outdated film. When he felt he had achieved his objective of thoroughly humiliating the photographer, he magnanimously declared that since there was not time to reschedule another shoot, he would have to deign to accept them and left it to me and the photographer to select which photos to submit with the article—subject to his final okay, of course.

The patently obvious motive for all this bullshit was of course, aside from his psychotic need to put everyone down, so that he could tell Chief Rourke that he, personally, had whipped the article into shape.

I'd already wined and dined the editor of the paper's Sunday supplement—who had previously been pressured by both my boss and the chief's aides—and confirmed that the piece would be the lead story the Sunday before the chief's press conference to announce his candidacy for governor.

On Thursday, C.C. called me into his office. I was praying that he was going to fire me, but no such luck. "Hardesty," he said, unwrapping a cigar about the size of a large zucchini, "this Rourke for Governor thing is going to put Carlton Carlson & Associates on the map. You didn't screw up the article assignment too badly…"

No greater praise…, I thought.

"… and I didn't hear any specific complaints about your attitude, so I'm going to let you keep handling future contacts with the family members. All direct contacts with the chief will, of course, be made by me and only me. With my help, Terrence

C. Rourke's going to be this state's next governor!" He banged his desk with one fist, then leaned forward to glare at me. "This is a big responsibility I'm giving you here, and you'd damned well better not fuck it up."

Why was I not thrilled? Why was I biting my tongue to keep from telling old C.C., there, to take his zucchini cigar and shove it up both his and the chief's ass? Why the hell didn't I just quit then and there? Why don't I have an answer for those last three questions? Suffice it to say, I was not thrilled, I held my tongue, and I swore to myself to start sending resumes out in the morning.

*   *   *

Friday night I spent sitting in front of the television, polishing off my third pack of cigarettes for the day. Chris went out with some friends from the store, and didn't get home until about two hours after the bars closed—a fact noted only because I'd gotten up to go to the bathroom just as he came in, and had looked at the clock.

What bothered me most about what I was beginning to see clearly as the approaching end of my relationship with Chris was that it really didn't scare me nearly as much as I thought it should. We still cared a lot for each other, I knew, but the kind of love that separates lovers from loving friends wasn't really there anymore. We'd just been growing in two different directions, and though we never talked about it, we both knew.

Anyway, on Saturday night we went to dinner—Chris insisted on Rasputin's again—and afterwards, the Ebony Room now gone, we decided to go back to Bacchus' Lair to catch the show. As if on cue, a pouring rain started just as we left the restaurant. *Two Saturdays in a row,* I told myself.

The place was packed; they'd installed a new maitre d' who unctuously informed us that without a reservation, we'd be lucky to get a seat at the bar. As we were deciding whether to take up his kind semi-offer or not, we heard a bellowed "Chile, there you are!" and looked toward the bar to see Tondelaya-nee-Teddy surging her way through the crowd. "I'll just bet you couldn't get a table, could you?" We both shook our heads in exact unison, looking, I'm sure, like the Synchronized Idiot team. She grabbed each of us by the arm and, before either of us could say anything, steered us past the maitre d' and into the room.

"My sister just called and told me she couldn't make it to the show tonight, so I'll put you at her table," T/T said, the rustle of her taffeta gown audible even above the hubbub of the crowd.

The table was so close to the stage we could, if we were so inclined—I for one certainly wasn't—look up the skirts of the performers. It was not near an exit. I looked at Chris who, reading my mind as he could so often do, grinned and shrugged.

Seeing us safely ensconced at the table, T/T blew us both poster-sized kisses and went to put finishing touches on her makeup before the show. The waiter came and took our drink order, then vanished into the crowd, hips expertly maneuvering between tables, extended arms and legs, and milling customers.

The table beside us was empty, but just as the music came on and the house lights started to dim, two forms were ushered up and seated by the maitre d'. I wasn't paying much attention until I heard: "Hi, Dick. Hi Chris," and looked over to see Bob Allen, owner of the recently burned out Ebony Room, and his lover, Ramón.

We returned the greeting—at least, I think we did; by that time we couldn't even hear our own voices over the always-tinny-sounding canned music—as the spotlight came on and the show began.

With a few variations, it was pretty much the same as the last time we'd seen it, except that T/T's rendition of "The Butcher's Son" seemed, if possible, a little raunchier than last time, and he made a point of directing the song to Chris and me.

At intermission, we had a chance, finally, to exchange a few words with Bob and Ramón. We'd finally spoken with Bob briefly on the phone some days before to express our regrets over the loss of the Ebony Room, but he'd been so busy we hadn't seen him since the fire.

"I didn't feel much like coming out tonight," Bob said, "but Ramón dragged me. I'm glad he did, actually—I'm not used to not being around a lot of people lately and I've kind of missed it. We almost didn't make it, though—had a hell of a time getting a cab in the rain."

"Something wrong with your car again?" I asked, and Bob snorted in disgust.

"The damned transmission this time. That lemon's been in the shop more than it's been on the road."

"Well, if you need a ride home after the show, we'll be glad to give you a lift," Chris volunteered.

"We'd appreciate that," Bob said.

*   *   *

It had stopped raining by the time we left the club, and most of the talk on the drive home was about Judy; her performance had been even better than the first time we'd seen her, and the crowd, again, was wild about her. But once again, she refused to come back for a curtain call, and Chris was speculating on whether her increasing popularity would change the situation.

"Don't count on it," Ramón volunteered from the back seat. "She's never done a curtain call, and if you ask me, she never will. That's one strange character, that Judy."

"Yeah, I'd been wondering about her," I said. "I think I've seen her around someplace as a guy, but I'm not sure—hard to tell with the wig and makeup. What's his real name?"

Ramón shrugged. "'Judy' is all I know," he said. "Nobody knows her. And I mean that literally. I worked there when the place first opened up—waiter, busboy, bartender; whatever they needed. Do you know that nobody in that place has ever seen her out of drag? Not only that, but nobody has ever seen her come in or go out? She doesn't mix with the other performers—hell, sometimes she doesn't even show up. Not often, granted, but…. She's got her own dressing room that she comes out of only when it's time for her to go on, and when the show's over, back in she goes, and that's it. You can stand outside that door all night, and you won't see her come out. Probably got a back door to her dressing room. Or maybe she lives there...who knows?"

"How can she manage that? Why the mystery and special treatment?" Chris asked.

Ramón shrugged. "Word has it she's sleeping with the manager—or the owner—or both."

"And who are the manager and the owner?" Chris asked.

"The manager's Dave Lee."

"And the owner?"

"Nobody seems to know. I think it's a corporation. If that's the case, Judy's a busy girl."

"Yeah," Bob said, "I know they don't belong to the Bar Guild."

We were pondering that little mystery as Chris pulled into the garage of our apartment building.

"You guys want to stop in for a drink?" Bob asked as we got on the elevator. "We owe you for the ride."

Chris looked to me, and I said "Sure; we'll have a quick one." I was curious to know more about Judy, and although I didn't want to pry into something that was really none of my business, I was hoping Bob would volunteer more information on the Ebony Room fire.

* * *

Chris asked for scotch, and I opted for coffee (decaf) and Strega, and settled down in their comfortable living room while Ramón took charge of fixing the coffee. Bob went to the beautiful mahogany hutch that served as a liquor cabinet and poured Chris's scotch and Strega for me, himself, and Ramón into beautiful leaded crystal glasses. When we were all seated—Bob in his favorite armchair and Ramón on the floor in front of him, leaning back against Bob's legs—the conversation turned to the series of fires plaguing the community's bars in general, and the fire at the Ebony Room in particular. Bob confirmed that someone had, indeed, tossed a Molotov cocktail through a small, high window in the bathroom. He figured it had happened about an hour after closing, shortly after the bartender had locked up for the night and gone home. The insurance company, of course, refused to settle the claim until it was determined that Bob himself had not started the fire. All evidence to the contrary, and the fact of there having been five other similar fires, the company remained adamant, and was giving Bob a hard time as it is the habit, duty, and delight of insurance companies to do.

"How is the investigation going?" I asked.

Bob shrugged. "Who knows? I've been calling the insurance company nearly every day and they keep saying they're still waiting for the arson report to come in—and of course hoping that when it does, it will implicate *me* as having set fire to my own place so they can deny the claim. I've made at least a dozen phone calls to both the fire department and the police, but it's pretty obvious they have more important things on their mind. I think the annual Firemen's and Policemen's Ball is coming up."

"Are you planning to reopen?" Chris asked.

Bob shrugged, one hand reaching out to tousle Ramón's hair. "Depends on what the insurance company does," he said. "I'd like to, of course—I own the building, or what's left of it, and I've been there ten years now. But even if the insurance comes through, they'll cancel me sure and it'll be next to impossible to get other insurance; especially with all these other bar fires lately. The Bar Guild is trying to pull something together, but I'm not sure what we can do.

"Being a bar owner isn't the easiest job in the world," he said, taking another sip of his Strega. "If it's not the fires, it's the police harassment, and with Chief Rourke at the helm, that's not likely to end soon."

"Careful what you say about Dick's good buddy," Chris said.

Bob looked at me quizzically, and I shot Chris a dirty look.

I sighed. "Mr. Tact, here, is referring to an assignment I've got shepherding our beloved chief and his family through the media minefields until he announces his candidacy for governor a week from Tuesday." Since the chief's political aspirations were common knowledge, I didn't feel I was betraying any confidences.

"Well, that ought to be a boon to the U-Haul and moving van industry," Bob said.

Ramón's eyes grew large. "You mean you actually know 'The Butcher'?" He gave a dramatic shudder. "I'm uncomfortable being on the same *planet* with that bigot—God knows what I'd do if I had to be in the same room. Does he know you're gay?"

It was my turn to shudder at the thought. "I sincerely doubt it," I said. "We're hardly what you'd call 'close'."

"I know his son," Bob said. "Knew him, I should say."

"His son's gay?" Ramón and Chris said in chorus.

Bob grinned. "You know, I *do* know a few people who aren't gay. But in this case, yeah. His son Pat was gay."

"Was?" Ramón said, turning to look up at Bob. "What did the chief do—have him castrated?"

"No," Bob said, "the chief had him killed."

CHAPTER 3

We all sat there for a moment in silence, absorbing the impact of Bob's little depth charge. Chris looked at me, gave a quick raise of his eyebrows, and drained his scotch.

Ramón finally broke the silence. "Had him killed? Are you serious?"

Bob shrugged. "So the story goes. I find it a little hard to believe, but it's been going around for years. The chief takes his two sons hunting in the mountains—rumor has it right after he found out Pat was gay—and only one son comes back."

"Just like that?" Chris asked, incredulous.

"Apparently so," Bob said. "They never did find Pat's body. The chief's story was that they'd split up and, when Pat didn't come back, the chief organized a search party which found Pat's gun at the edge of a bluff. There'd been heavy rains, and they figured Pat was standing near the edge of the bluff when part of it broke off and fell into the river below."

"Wow," Ramón said, almost in a whisper.

"Yeah, wow," I said. "But that raises an interesting question aside from whatever happened to Patrick."

"What's that?" Chris asked.

"The chief's sons were twins," I found myself saying. "Identical twins. If one was gay, wouldn't it be a pretty strong bet the other would be gay, too?"

"I'd think so, of course," Chris volunteered. "But there haven't been any really definitive studies done yet on sexual preference in identical twins, though I don't know why. It would make a fascinating study."

"I didn't know that bastard even had kids," Ramón interjected, "until I saw a picture in the paper of the one who got married a year or so ago. If Bob weren't around, that guy could put his shoes under my bed any day." He shot a quick glance at Bob, who playfully swatted him on the back of the head with the flat of his hand.

"That's Kevin," I said. "Patrick's twin, and I guess he is pretty attractive now that I think of it. When I met him I was only thinking of how to get through the afternoon with the chief, which didn't leave much time for admiring the scenery."

"Well, that settles the sexual preference question," Ramón said, his face and voice taking on a professorial tone. "The brother's married; he can't be gay. I think I read that somewhere."

Chris and I just looked at each other, and Bob pulled Ramón toward him in a bear hug and said, in his best fatherly voice: "You'll have to excuse the lad—when he fell off the turnip truck I'm afraid he landed on his head." Ramón growled and bent his head forward to bite Bob on the wrist.

"It occurs to me," Bob said, after removing his arm from Ramón's attack, "that if I knew, or suspected, that my old man had bumped off my brother because he was gay, I just might think about straightening myself out real fast."

We small-talked for another twenty minutes or so until I noticed Chris and Ramón stifling yawns and said: "I think it's time we went home." Bob and Ramón got up to walk us to the door, and on the way, Bob put his hand on my shoulder.

"Do you remember the guy you were dating when you first started coming into the Ebony Room—just before you met Prince Charming, here?"

I nodded. "Tom. Tom Erickson. Yeah. I was still in college."

"And do you remember what Tom Erickson did for a living?"

I thought a moment. "He was a fireman."

Bob looked at me, left eyebrow raised. "*Noooo*, not just a fireman. He was on the…" he paused, his eyebrow continuing to raise until it almost lost itself in his hair line, coaxing me to remember what I probably never should have forgotten. A light went on in my head.

"He was on the *arson* squad," I said. "Still is, last I heard."

"Bingo!" Bob said.

"And you would like me to call him after not having talked to him in five years to see if he knows anything about the bar fires." I wasn't quite sure it was a good idea, but at the same time I was a little embarrassed for not at least having thought of it myself.

"I'd hang up on you," Chris said.

"You have," I noted. "Many times. But let's not rattle the skeletons just now."

Chris slowly brought up his fist until it was about six inches in front of my face and slowly unfurled the middle finger.

I just as slowly brought my right hand forward from my side, fingers spread wide, grabbed his crotch, and squeezed. Chris yelped and dropped his fist. "Bastard," he said with a grin.

"Are they friends, daddy?" Ramón asked Bob.

"I think so," Bob said, then addressed himself to me. "I'd really appreciate it," he said. "I'd have called him myself, but I didn't really know him all that well and I wouldn't want to put him in an awkward position. As I remember, he was pretty closeted."

"Only at work," I said, "and I certainly wouldn't call him there. But you're right: I imagine if there's anything to know, he just might be the one to know it."

Chris, leaning against the half open door, lowered his chin to his chest and made a 'come on, come on' gesture with one hand.

"Okay, okay, I'm coming." I said as he closed his eyes and made a loud snoring sound. "I'll give Tom a call tomorrow," I told Bob. "Thanks for the drink, guys."

Chris grabbed me by the sleeve and pulled me out into the hall as Bob and Ramón waved good night.

*   *   *

After having spent a week slaving in the cotton fields for old Massah C.C., and anticipating the week to come, I would

have preferred just to have spent Sunday vegetating, but I'd told
Bob I'd call Tom, so I felt obligated to do it, though I put it off
until after noon. Tom was a good guy, actually, but we'd more
or less lost contact with one another after I met Chris. We
probably could have gone on to be friends, but Chris and I are
both Scorpios, and Scorpios are notorious for waging a
continuous—and most generally losing—battle with jealousy.
Starting a new relationship is hard enough under the best of
circumstances, and I didn't want to give Chris any unnecessary
cause for concern, so Tom and I just sort of closed the door
between us. He had met someone almost immediately after, I
heard, and had moved out to the suburbs. I really felt a little
guilty at not having maintained contact with him and I hoped,
as I put out my umpteenth cigarette of the day and reached for
the phone book, that he wouldn't think it too odd for me to call
now.

Fortunately, he was listed, and with some trepidation, I
dialed his number. The phone was answered on the second ring
by a rich, masculine voice I recognized immediately.

"Tom?" I verified. "This is a voice from your far distant
past—too far, I'm ashamed to say; Dick Hardesty."

"Dick! My God, what a surprise! It's good to hear from you."
He sounded as though he meant it, and I was glad. "How have
you been? Are you still with Chuck?"

"Chris," I said, "and yes, we're still at it. How about you?"

"Single again, I'm sad to say. Kent—I don't think you ever
met him, did you?—was just too…well, too open about who he
was. He could never understand why I had to be so 'uptight' as
he called it. I hate having to walk a tightrope all the time, but
I had too much invested with my job to risk throwing it all
away."

"You're still with the department, then?" I asked.

Tom sighed. "Yeah. There just aren't too many openings
in the private sector for an arson investigator."

"As a matter of fact, Tom, I was kind of hoping to talk with
you about something having to do with the department, if it

wouldn't be improper for you to do it."

"Ah," he said, "so this isn't just a social call?" Fortunately, I recognized the teasing tone in his voice, but I still felt embarrassed.

"Well, uh," I mumbled, hoping I didn't sound as flustered as I felt; "let's say it's both." I felt not unlike a kid caught with his hand in the cookie jar, and I could have kicked myself for not having been more diplomatic. But, then, tact was never one of my strong points.

"That's okay," Tom said, sensing my awkwardness. "I'm still glad you called."

"Me, too," I said, and meant it. I guess I'd forgotten just how well the two of us had gotten along. "Listen," I said, "why don't we get together; maybe you can come over for dinner some night this week?"

"Yeah, that might be nice. But I tell you what: I'm free later this afternoon. Would you and Chris like to join me for a drink? You know I'm not much of a bar person, but I've got to come into town, and I've been having the urge to stop in somewhere for one. I hate drinking alone."

"Sounds good to me," I said. "Let me check with Chris." I put my hand over the receiver and yelled to Chris in the bathroom. "You feel up to going out for a drink with Tom this afternoon?"

"Can't," Chris called back. "It's bowling day, remember? You go ahead if you want."

I shrugged and took my hand from off the mouthpiece. "I forgot," I told Tom; "Chris has bowling this afternoon. But I'd still like to get together, if we can make it fairly early. Tomorrow's back-to-the-grind day."

"Sure," Tom said. "It's what…one thirty now." I checked my watch. He was right. "How about 3:30 or 4:00?"

"Fine with me," I said, cradling the phone under one ear while lighting up another cigarette. "Where?"

"Calypso's? About 3:30, then?"

I might have guessed. Calypso's was very popular with those

with, for whatever reason, one foot in the closet; businessmen, rising young executives, up-and-coming arson investigators. Three-piece suits were *de rigeur* weekdays during cocktail hour, though on Sundays the dress code was a bit more relaxed. The Sunday brunch crowd was almost exclusively though discreetly gay, the clientele switching to almost completely straight by mid evening.

"Great," I said. "I'll see you there."

Fortunately I'd already gone through my hour-long shower ritual when I'd first gotten up. I usually tried to get up before Chris even opened his eyes so I could be more than halfway through my shower before he started pounding on the shower door complaining about the water bill. Like our Saturday night dinners, it was one of those little family rituals we'd developed over the years.

Chris had joined a gay bowling league a few months earlier; I think maybe in part because he knew I didn't care for the game and it gave him a chance to flirt without having to feel guilty. I also suspected he might be chalking up a few strikes with at least one of his teammates but, as I said earlier, our relationship had reached the point where it didn't bother even an old Scorpio like me nearly as much as it once would have.

*   *   *

I was, as usual, early. Even at 3:15 on a Sunday afternoon the bar was fairly crowded. There was a strong contingent left over from brunch, getting progressively but still discreetly more smashed as the afternoon wore on. Although things were beginning to loosen up, discretion was still the better part of valor. Should the "g" word be spoken audibly enough for others to hear, stern looks would be cast in the direction of the offender. I found the whole elaborate charade more than a little silly, which probably accounted for my seldom coming into the place.

Tom did not arrive until my second Bloody Mary was pretty well gone. I was watching for him in the mirror behind the bar, and spotted him as he wove his way through a clot of good-bye sayers at the door. Of course, Tom's red-blond hair would have stood out even if he weren't nearly six-foot-six. Not having seen him for five years, I was struck by the fact that he was still as attractive as ever, and that his hair was thinning noticeably.

He spotted me watching him in the mirror, gave a big grin and, expertly dodging a waiter with a tray full of drinks, came up to pat me resoundingly on the back. I turned around on my stool and we shook hands. At any other gay bar, we'd probably have hugged.

"Now, as I was saying…," he said.

"Oh, come on," I replied, "it's only been five years."

"The merest flicker of an angel's eyelash," he said, grinning again.

Tom caught the bartender's attention and ordered a scotch rocks. "You ready for another one?"

"Why not?" I replied and the bartender nodded his head and moved off to make the drinks.

"Sorry to hear about you and Kent," I said.

Tom shrugged. "It happens," he said. "Glad you're still with Chuck….sorry, *Chris*…though."

It was my turn to shrug. "Yeah, but I don't think it'll be for too much longer." I caught myself by surprise with that one: I usually keep my private problems pretty much private.

Tom pulled a bill out of his wallet and exchanged it for our drinks, waving away the proffered change. "Sorry," he said.

"Like you say, it happens. And it's not so much that we're 'breaking up' as it is that we've just sort of drifted apart. I think we'll always stay friends."

We were both quiet for a minute, staring into our drinks. "So," I said finally, "fill me in on the last five years." Boy, did that sound stupid! Have another drink, Hardesty!

Tom grinned. "I was thinking about that on the way over here, and I was really surprised to come to the conclusion that other than my relatively brief relationship with Kent, nothing much at all has changed since the last time we saw one another.

Not much to say for five years, is it?"

"Your job going okay?" I asked.

"So-so. I took the test for promotion last month. Didn't make it, but there's always next time, right?" He couldn't quite hide a note of bitterness. "And I still love doing what I do."

I gave a deep sigh and took the celery stick out of my Bloody Mary, tapping the end on the rim of the glass to keep it from dripping. "Wish to hell I could say the same," I said, taking a healthy and very loud bite of celery. "I'm stuck in a shit job with an asshole for a boss…but other than that, everything's great."

This wasn't going quite the way I'd have liked it to.

"So what did you want to talk to me about, as if I didn't have a pretty good idea?" Tom asked.

"The fires." I said, feeling a little awkward for imposing on a friend.

"That's what I do for a living. I'm in the fire department. Would you like to see my badge?" Tom said with a small grin. "You'll have to be a little more specific as to which fires."

I couldn't help but grin. "You bastard—you know damned good and well which fires."

Tom looked off toward the back of the restaurant. "Is the patio still open? Maybe we can find a table out there. A little less noisy."

And a lot more private, I intuited. "Good idea," I said, as I got off the stool and picked up my drink to follow Tom through the restaurant part of the bar.

The patio was open, and there were quite a few empty tables. Tom picked out one surrounded by other empty tables, and we sat down. "Better," he said, and I nodded in agreement.

"You know that I really shouldn't be talking to you—or to anybody else—about this. It's department business, and they're pretty strict about not leaking information on ongoing cases."

I felt like a total asshole. He was right, of course. "Look, Tom," I started to say; "I'm…"

But Tom held up his hand to silence me. "First let me ask you why you're wanting to know whatever it is you want to know?"

I explained to him about Bob and the Ebony Room, and how everything seemed to be hanging on the arson report, and that Bob just wanted to know what was going on and couldn't get any information at all through the regular channels.

Tom sat staring into his drink as I talked. When I finished, he remained silent, then suddenly sighed and looked up at me.

"Did you know I was a fag, Dick?"

Now, *that* I wasn't expecting! "Did I *what*?" I asked, not sure that I heard him correctly.

"I asked if you knew I was a fag." He put one open hand over his chin, and moved it slowly down to his neck, as if he were checking for beard stubble. "*I* didn't. I knew I was gay, but I didn't know I was a fag."

I just sat there, a puzzled look on my face, waiting for him to continue.

Tom took another sip of his drink, put the glass down, and took up his story: "I told you I took the promotions test last month, and that I didn't get it. And while I was really disappointed, I figured 'Hey, it happens.' And then a couple days after the test, I had to go down to the main office for some paperwork, and stopped in the john. I was in one of the stalls and just pulling my pants up when I heard two guys come in, and they were talking about the test. One of them mentioned my name and said something like 'I was surprised Erickson didn't make it;' and the other guy said 'I heard it was because they don't promote fags,' and they laughed.

"They might as well have come in and spit in my face. Man, I stormed out of that stall like a bull into the arena and went right up to them. 'What the *fuck* are you talking about?' I said. I guess I surprised the shit out of them—the one guy I knew looked really embarrassed and the other one just sort of stammered something I couldn't hear. 'Speak up, you stupid shit!' I yelled at him. 'Where did you hear anybody say I was a fag?' I was so fucking pissed I couldn't see straight, and they damned well knew it. The guy was sort of backed up against the washbasins with his head pulled back away from me, like he was afraid I was going to hit him, which I was just about ready to do.

"'I just heard a couple of the examiners talking after they'd finished the grading,' the guy said, 'and I heard your name and that they don't promote fags. Shit, man, *I* didn't say you were a fag. I don't even *know* you.' I was forcing myself to pull back a little bit, but I said: 'That's fucking right, you don't. But *I* know *you* now and if I hear anybody else saying I'm a fag—and I mean *anybody*—I'm coming looking for *you*, and you damn well better believe it.' And then I turned around and walked out the door."

I was impressed, and it must have shown on my face. "That took one hell of a lot of guts," I said. "I'm really proud of you!"

Tom just shrugged, and said "Thanks." Then he drained his glass and set it on the table. He fished out an ice cube with one finger and put it in his mouth.

"I probably should have let it drop right there," he said after a minute, "but I didn't. I went in to see my chief and told him I knew damned well I'd done better on the exam than anybody else, and I wanted to know exactly why I didn't make the promotion list. My chief's a good guy, and a decent one, too. He gave me a couple lame excuses that I could tell he didn't believe himself. But as I was leaving, he said 'Tom, take my advice and don't make waves. You're a good arson investigator—one of the best. But there are just certain things you can't change. And I don't want you to jeopardize your job.' And I knew exactly what he was referring to.

"So it boils down to this: if I keep my mouth shut and just let them shit on me whenever they feel like it, I can keep my job. But I'm as far up the ladder as I'm ever going to get."

I shook my head in empathy/sympathy.

"So that's why I decided to talk to you," he said, fishing another ice cube from his glass. "I've got to tell you I was more than a little unhappy with you when you took up with Chris and dropped me like a hot potato. I thought we were better friends than that."

I started to say something, but he put his hand up to stop me.

"That's all water under the bridge," he said. "But when you called, I suspected you wanted to know about the bar fires—you always were a nosy bastard, you know." He grinned at me, and the best I could muster was a weak half-smile.

"But I figured I've worked my ass off for the department for seven years; I've been tiptoeing around this gay thing all that time, and realize now that my breaking up with Kent had a large part to do with my believing that staying locked in the closet would protect me. And it didn't. I'm not going to live my life like that anymore. I can't."

I nodded again. "There'll come a time when you won't have to," I said. "I don't know when that'll be, but things are starting to change. I suspect Stonewall just might be our 'shot heard 'round the world'. At least I hope so."

I finished my Bloody Mary and pointed to the empty glasses in an unasked question. Tom shook his head. "Enough for me, I think," he said. "So—ask away."

"Well, first, when is the department going to release whatever they know to the insurance companies? I imagine Bob Allen's not the only bar owner out there whose life is pretty much in limbo. The insurance companies don't give a shit, of course— every day their money sits in the bank, they're getting interest on it."

"Well," Tom said, "as far as the department's official stand, they don't want to release any information to anybody, including the insurance companies, until they have dotted all the 'I's and crossed the 't's. They're just applying this 'policy' a little more stringently to the bar fires. And if the bar owners have to wait, who cares? The longer those fag bars stay closed, the safer our streets will be for *decent* people."

"Huh?" I asked. Tom just grinned and shrugged.

"Well," I said, "what about the basics? Do they or do they not know who's behind the fires? And are they all linked to one source—as I'd imagine they all have to be? I noticed that what little media coverage there has been has given the impression that they're all just spontaneous, random acts of moral outrage against an uppity gay community's daring to think it has rights like other people."

"Yeah, they pretty much know. I've been on about 2/3 of the bar fires, and they're strictly by the numbers. Molotov cocktails using a Valley Vineyards Chianti bottle with the label removed—which is stupid as hell, because it's the only bottle with that shape—long neck, extra wide base. I suspect he does that just so we'll be sure to know it's him. And in case you might think his choice of wines might be a clue, I should point out that Valley Vineyards Chianti is available in 2/3 of the city's liquor stores, and 1/4 to 1/3 of the restaurants. He's a pretty vain bastard who really gets a kick out of thumbing his nose at us. Rag wick from an old 180-thread-count white sheet; all the arsonist's little personal trademarks which were known only to him and to us. Oh, yes, and all tossed in back windows between 3 and 5:30 in the morning. The Main didn't have a back window, so they tossed it on the roof. Oh, and if the window is barred and the bars are too close together to fit the bottle through, he breaks the window and uses the extra long neck of the bottle to pour the gas down the inside wall. Then he leaves the bottle sitting on the ground under the window, where we'll be sure to find it. No fingerprints, of course."

"So they do know who did it?" I asked.

Tom nodded. "Sure—it's the classic M.O. of a well-known fire-for-pay professional by the name of Jerry Tamasini."

He was quiet a minute, apparently waiting for me to say something. "*And…?*" I said. "…are there any plans to arrest Mr. Tamasini any time soon?"

Tom picked up his glass and tipped it back to get at the last piece of ice at the bottom. He munched it loudly and, after swallowing, said: "They don't have to. He's currently serving 25-to-life down state. Been there two years now."

I sat there looking at him without speaking for much longer than I intended. Finally, I managed to say: "Then why the charade? If whoever is doing this knows damned well that the police will recognize the M.O. and know Tamasini's in jail...."

Tom smiled. "Well, there is the fairly reasonable theory that he somehow has an apprentice on the outside. But I personally feel that Tamasini has way too big an ego to share his little trademarks with anyone else. But the police and most of the arson squad prefer the apprentice theory to the other, more realistic one."

"Which is?" I asked.

"Which is that the arsonist is thumbing his nose at us, letting us know he knows that the police and arson squad know. I think he may be telling us he's one of us."

CHAPTER 4

Tom and I left the bar shortly after our conversation about the fires and my sincere apologies for having been such a jerk in not maintaining our friendship. I assured him that I would use utmost discretion in whatever information I passed on, and of course promised not to reveal my source (Bob, of course, already knew). He made me swear that I wouldn't tell the specifics of Tamasini's M.O.—which had never been made public and were supposedly only known by Tamasini, the arson squad, and a selected group of department bigwigs. That it could actually be someone in the fire or police departments…. I called Bob Allen as soon as I got home and told him what little I could: basically, that he shouldn't expect to be taking an insurance check to the bank any time soon, but that he definitely didn't have to worry about anyone thinking he'd torched his own bar. I told him I'd keep him posted on anything I might find out or hear later down the line.

Tom was right—I *was* "nosy"; if something piqued my curiosity, I couldn't stop niggling at it until I got an answer. And I found myself niggling.

I'd was slouched in my chair in front of the TV, surrounded by full ashtrays, thinking about what Tom had said and its implications, when Chris came in from bowling—at 10:45. They'd had the lanes reserved from 5 'til 7.

He seemed surprised to see me still up. "Sorry I'm so late," he said. "I should have called, but I figured you and Tom had a lot to catch up on, and I ran into a couple guys from the store, so we went out for a couple drinks." More than a couple, I'd judge, from the faint odor of alcohol that trailed after him as he went into the bedroom and started undressing for bed. He continued talking to me through the open door. "There's a hot rumor going around that Marston's is being bought out by some big chain in New York. That should be interesting. I sure hope they don't come in and start replacing the entire staff—especially the head window designer, of course.

"How about you? Find out anything from Tom about the fires?"

"Not enough," I said as I put out my cigarette, turned off the TV and the lights, and went into the bedroom to join Chris.

*   *   *

The following week was a very busy one. Monday and Tuesday were spent taking care of a million details leading up to Chief Rourke's press conference the following week—details for which, as with the forthcoming newspaper article, C.C. of course took full credit. A phone call from the chief came in while C.C.'s secretary and I were in his office going over our respective responsibilities on C.C.'s checklist, which was only a few pages shorter than "War and Peace." Rather than shooing us out of the office with a disdainful wave of his hand, he deigned to let us stay while he oiled his way into the chief's good graces.

"Why, yes, Chief, " C.C. said, leaning back in his chair and swiveling it around so he had his back to us. "Yes, the article will definitely appear in this Sunday's edition, and I did a pretty good job on it, if I do say so myself. I'm sure you'll agree. Yes...yes... I've seen to that...and that too...yes, and I'm working on that right now. You don't have to worry about a thing, Chief; I spent the entire weekend here in the office, working, but I've got it all covered. Yes, and I'll look forward to our 4:00 meeting tomorrow."

C.C.'s secretary and I exchanged glances, and she rolled her eyes to the ceiling. If old C.C. spent the weekend in the office, it sure as hell wasn't because he was working—office gossip was that whenever his wife and kid were out of town for the weekend, as they had been the past weekend, C.C. spent every waking hour on the fancy leather couch in his office, boinking some bimbo from Accounting.

On Wednesday, Chris announced that Marston's had, indeed, been bought out by the New York chain, that the place had been swarming with New York bigwigs, and that he had been scheduled for an interview with one of them on Thursday afternoon. He was firmly convinced the ax was about to fall, though I assured him that any other store in town would kill to have him join them.

And on Thursday morning, I was summoned into C.C.'s office and, for the first time in memory, offered a chair. That magnanimous gesture, I was sure, boded no good. I sat down carefully on the edge of the chair, lest wrist bands suddenly spring from the arms and a metal cap with thick electrical wiring drop over my head.

"Hardesty," C.C. said in his pseudo-sincere, bullshitting-the-clients voice, "I've got some great news, which *could* be great news for you, too, if you're half as smart as you think you are. I wanted to talk to you first because if you're stupid enough to pass this up, I'll have to find somebody else, and I'm not going to have you embarrass me by turning it down later."

The silver tongued devil. I leaned even further forward, waiting for the switch to be thrown.

"Carlton Carlson & Associates has been appointed official public relations firm for Chief Rourke's campaign for governor!" He said, proudly. "All the legwork, all the liaison between the chief and his various teams, and the full P.R. package. And I've decided to let *you* be part of it. In fact, I'm thinking of appointing you my special assistant for the length of this project!"

Which was to say that *I* would be doing all the legwork and the liaison, and the bulk of the full P.R. package would be sitting on my desk while C.C. did all the ass kissing and the oiling up and the squeezing of every ounce of credit for everything that went right. And, of course, if something should happen to go wrong, C.C. would have a convenient scapegoat for the blame: me.

Well, I'd played C.C.'s little games just about long enough, and I decided it was time I took control of my own life. There were other jobs out there, and I could find one easily enough. Not one that paid anywhere near what I was making, probably, but money isn't everything.

"Well, thanks, Mr. Carlson," I said. "I really appreciate your trust in me" (I actually said that! And I didn't burst out laughing!), "but I think I'm going to have to pass on your offer."

C.C. looked at me like I'd just put a gerbil in the microwave. No one...*no one* in the employ of Carlton Carlson & Associates *ever* said "no" to Carlton Carlson, because if they did, they were automatically no longer in the employ of Carlton Carlson & Associates.

He stared at me for a full minute while I prayed for death.

"How much am I paying you?" he said, finally. I told him.

"For the length of this assignment, I will increase that amount by 15 percent."

Something very strange was going on here, and I decided that since I had already jumped off the roof and was passing the 15th floor on my way down, I didn't have too much to lose.

"Twenty-five percent," I said. He looked like Zeus had just walked up and slapped him across the side of his head with a thunderbolt. I actually saw him shudder.

But he pulled himself together and after looking at me through narrowed eyes, which made my skin crawl, nodded and said "Deal. And we'll put that in writing, so that there won't be any further...negotiations...in the future. An increase in salary of 25 percent between today and the end of this assignment." Which I knew perfectly well would also be the end of my employment.

Realizing that I may well be pushing my luck a bit too far, I said: "May I ask why you selected me for this assignment?"

C.C. sat back in his chair and once again became Mr. Professional. "Chief Rourke will be continuing his duties as Chief of Police during the campaign and has appointed his son, Kevin, to be his spokesman whenever possible. Kevin, it seems, has inexplicably been impressed by your handling of your limited dealings with the family thus far as a representative of this firm, and specifically requested that you keep on in that capacity. The chief concurs. You will meet with Kevin at that homeless shelter he runs over at 16th and Boyle tomorrow afternoon at 3 p.m. to see how you can best be of assistance to him. And let me make it very clear that whatever Kevin wants, you will provide. And you will of course keep me informed in detail of *everything* that goes on."

C.C. pulled another huge cigar out of the thermidor on his desk. And gave a slight flick of his free hand in my direction. "That's all for now," he said.

I got up to leave, my legs feeling oddly tingly, and had the door part-way open before C.C.'s voice caught me.

"And Hardesty," he said, lighting his cigar and blowing a long stream of smoke into the room, "I do not take kindly to intimidation of *any* kind."

"Yes, sir," I said as I let myself out.

Kevin, eh? I thought.

*   *   *

I got home a little before Chris, as usual, and went about making the basic preparations for dinner, setting the table, etc..

I can say I did it, but I wasn't really aware of it at the time. I kept wondering who had suckered whom today and the answer was fairly clear that once again C.C. had really pulled all the strings. He got his scapegoat, and I felt just a little bit like Judas—only the one I'd sold out was me. And I was more than a little curious about this Kevin thing. I had hardly done enough to qualify as an invaluable assistant—I had never said more than 10 words to Kevin. But there were those eye-contact/eye-evasion things. And if Patrick had been gay, was it not possible that Kevin…?

My thoughts were interrupted by the sound of Chris coming in the front door. He walked into the kitchen, said "Hi" and went directly to the freezer for ice. "Want one?" he asked, as he reached into the glass cupboard.

"I was just waiting for you," I said.

I noticed that he seemed a little…uncomfortable?…ill at ease?….hard to say; I just could sense that something was going on.

He fixed our drinks and handed mine to me. "How was your day?" he asked. He had a very un-Chris look on his face and there was a tightness in his voice.

"It can wait," I said. "I think I should hear about *your* day, first. Lets go into the living room." We found our way to the sofa and, as usual, sat side by side. We both set our drinks on the coffee table at the same time, in the same movement. That happened a lot.

"So," I said, putting my hand on his leg, "tell. You got the ax?"

Chris looked at me, and I thought he might start to cry. "No," he said.

"Well, that's *great*" I said, and meant it. "But something's wrong… what?"

Chris bit his lower lip and swept his thumb across the corner of his eye. "They offered me a promotion," he said. I couldn't understand why that should make him cry.

"And…?" I said, knowing there was something else.

"They want me to move to New York," he said. "I told them I couldn't give them an answer right away. I had to talk to you first. It's a big raise, and a fantastic opportunity. But they want me to be there ready to start on the first of the month. And…"

"Then I think you should take it if you want it," I said, and rubbed my hand up and down the top of his thigh. I couldn't describe exactly what I was feeling—a mixture of happiness for Chris, and sadness for us, and an odd loneliness for me.

"Would you come with me?" he asked, and I could sense that while he meant it, he didn't mean it 100 percent—he knew, as I did, that it was time for us to move on.

"I can't right now," I said, and told him about the commitment I'd made to C.C. "Maybe when this campaign thing is over, if you want me to...."

We each leaned toward the other, and hugged, tightly. Chris put his head on my shoulder and started to sob; I had a lump the size of a grapefruit in my throat, and my vision was suddenly very blurry, but I patted him on the back as if I were comforting a sad, small child.

"I'll miss you," he said, and started sobbing again.

"No more than I'll miss you," I said, and truly meant it. We were five years of the other's life; goodbyes are never easy.

*   *   *

Friday morning was more or less a total blur. Fortunately, it was a relatively easy morning—mostly involving assembling and collating materials for the press kit to be handed out just before Chief Rourke's announcement of his candidacy. All I could really think about was Chris, and Chris and me, and how fast life can change so totally. It was probably a good thing that C.C. was out of the office most of the morning, and I have the vague recollection that he didn't even look in my direction when he finally stormed in, barking orders like a drill sergeant to various members of the staff.

I did remember my 3 o'clock appointment with Kevin, however, and left the office with more than enough time to spare in getting there. 16th & Boyle sounded awfully familiar, but I had no idea why—it was, not surprisingly for the location of a homeless shelter, in one of the less fashionable areas of town, and it wasn't until I was only a block or so away that I realized that Bacchus' Lair was a half a block down from 16th on Arnwood, and Boyle was the next street down, Now there's an ironic bit of coincidence, I thought.

Finding a parking place was no problem in this area— being sure your car would still be there in one piece when you came back for it was another story. Not usually a problem for the bars along Arnwood, there was plenty of traffic at night. But just one block away it was a bit more risky.

The Salvation's Door shelter was a sprawling, dilapidated four-story former God-knows-what. Its original floor level facade had been replaced by a solid brick-and-concrete-block wall, broken only by the narrow, recessed double-solid-slab-door entrance, over which was hung a large, brightly painted plywood sign proclaiming that this was, indeed, Salvation's Door.

The street was pretty much deserted, and there was no one around the entrance—it was much too early for the overnight guests, and the evening meal wouldn't be served for a few hours yet. It looked like the place might well be locked up, but when I tried the door, it opened easily, leading me immediately into a long corridor broken by numerous doors and openings. Directly to the left of the entry was a wide stairway, going up, with a sign beside it on the wall saying: "Registration: 2nd Floor." I gathered that was where the dormitory rooms were. There were no sounds coming from upstairs, so I assumed there would be no one there at this time of day.

No one seemed to be around on the ground floor, either, though since I could hear kitchen-type sounds from somewhere in the back, I just kept walking in that direction, glancing to the left and right as I passed each door/opening. A large room with chairs and a pulpit to the right; a couple smaller rooms set up apparently as meeting rooms; a few offices. A wide arch about three quarters of the way down on the right led into a vast dining area lined with tables. The kitchen was, I assumed, directly to the rear of it. At the very end of the corridor, a stairway to the left led upwards, and a sign said simply "Director, Second Floor". I climbed the stairs and found a truncated hallway, off which there was only one partially opened door, with a sign: "Director". I knocked, and a voice I vaguely recognized said "Come in."

Kevin Rourke was seated behind a very old, very large and heavy-looking desk piled high with papers, file folders, those large accordion-type manila envelopes with strings to tie them shut, and books. Behind him was an equally large bulletin board covered with notes, business cards, official looking operating permits of one sort or another, handwritten notes, etc. On the wall beside the bulletin board was a framed 8x10 color photo of a smiling Kevin standing behind and with a loving hand—the left hand, of course, to prominently display his wedding ring—on the shoulder of a seated, smiling Sue-Lynn, holding a smiling Sean. In one corner of the small room was, inexplicably, a battered upright piano, atop which was an expensive looking tape recorder and an open bible.

Kevin rose and came around the desk to shake my hand. He had a very firm grasp and I was keenly aware that he held the handshake just a fraction of a second longer than necessary. "Mr. Hardesty," he said, with a very engaging smile; "I'm really glad you could come. Please, sit…" And he bent over to take a stack of folders off one of the heavy wooden chairs sitting sideways in front of the desk, then moved to a second and repeated the process. He laid the combined stack on one side of the already cluttered desk as I sat down. He then pulled the second chair over directly in front of me, and sat himself, our knees within about 6 inches of touching. He leaned forward, resting his elbows on the wooden arms of his chair and clasping his hands.

"We haven't really haven't had much of a chance to talk, have we?"

"No," I admitted, "we haven't." For some reason, I kept hearing the little gaydar in my head going "*Ping! Ping! Ping!*" With absolutely no evidence to support it, other than what I realized with mild surprise was possibly my own wishful thinking, I forced my mind to turn it off. Kevin Rourke was a pretty hot number, but business is business, and never the twain…etc.

"I hope you don't mind my asking, Mr. Hardesty…"

"Please, call me Dick," I interrupted.

Kevin smiled. "…Dick, but are you a Christian?"

Well, THIS was a brief assignment, I said to myself. But I wasn't about to lie, job or no job. "I'm a practicing agnostic," I said.

Kevin's smile did not fade by a single degree. "No matter," he said. "We're all God's children. I just thought that if you were…more spiritually oriented…we might start our meeting—and our working relationship—with a brief prayer for my father and the success of his campaign."

I'd rather have bamboo slivers driven under my fingernails, I thought.

"Well, then," Kevin said, still smiling, "let's get down to business, shall we?"

"Fine," I said, relieved that he didn't seem to take offense at being in the presence of a heathen. "Did you have some specific ideas, Reverend?"

Had Kevin been able to purse his lips and smile at the same time, I'm sure he would have. But he gave up the latter for the former, and leaned back in his chair. "Kevin, please," he said. "We're not unaware," he continued, "that my father has a…well, let's say a less than positive image in the minds of far too many of the people he will need in order to win the election. I propose that we start there—getting the public to see my father as a deeply caring and spiritual man."

Are we talking about the same guy, here? I wondered, but of course said nothing.

"Were you aware, for example, that this building belongs to my father, and that he donated it to the Shelter's use? He did it with no publicity whatever, but merely out of a sincere Christian desire to help those unfortunate souls who find themselves in need—in no small part as a result of the economic policies of the present governor."

Who the hell IS this guy? I wondered. *Mixing Christian good works and politics in the same breath?*

"Well," I said, "perhaps that might be a good place to start: what about having a fund-raiser held here at the shelter? It would be a great way for your father and his supporters to show their deep concern for the homeless, and an opportunity for the public to see that your father is more than just a cipher in a Chief of Police uniform ."

My ears couldn't believe how totally hypocritical my mouth seemed to be. How in hell could I even think of working for such a bigoted asshole—two, if you counted the chief and C.C., which I did—and keep any shred of personal dignity?

Well, I was actually coming to see myself as a resistance fighter, and realized it might be possible, by working from within, to throw a couple well-placed monkey wrenches into the chief's political machinery.

The fund-raiser idea was a win-win situation. First, the chief needed something like this if he had any chance of showing a human side—which I doubted he could pull off successfully, if our first meeting was any indication. He might come across as remotely warm and fuzzy in the Sunday supplement, where every word was doctored and every photo staged, but put him in with real people in a real life situation? Second, there was no way in hell that the chief's upper crust supporters would be seen dead in a dump like this without some major cosmetic improvements being made first, which could be of actual benefit to the homeless who used its facilities. Third, in the very remote possibility they might not see the depth-charge potential of the visual contrast of tuxedos and rags in the same room at the same time, I suspected a lot of the voters would. Fourth, if they acceded to holding a fund-raiser in the shelter but without having to actually be in the same room with anyone not on the city's social register, it would almost inevitably mean that the shelter would have to close down for a short period while the fund-raiser was being set up and held. In that event, an anonymous tip to the local media on the day of the gala could be devastating to the campaign.

Kevin appeared conflicted. "Well, Dick, my father is really not accustomed to actually dealing with the public in any numbers. He is a very private person."

"Kevin," I said, realizing I might be a little too forward, but not really caring, "since I work for the public relations firm charged with doing everything possible to get your father elected, I hope you will allow me to be honest—and blunt."

Kevin nodded. "Of course," he said.

"The hard cold fact is that the potential governor of a state cannot shut himself off from the people whom he plans to represent and whose support he needs to win. Your father, to be very blunt, has a reputation—however unfair it may be—of being aloof and patrician. If the only votes that counted were those of his backers, who are almost without exception the wealthy of this community, there would be no contest. But since the poor and middle class will also be voting, and still outnumber the wealthy by a considerable margin, he has to win them over, uncomfortable as it might be to him."

Kevin smiled. "I appreciate your candor, Dick," he said. "That's why I suggested to my father that you and I work together…closely. I was watching you during your visit to my parents' home: I could see you weren't intimidated by the situation or the surroundings. And I'll also be blunt in saying that while Mr. Carlson is undoubtedly a very capable P.R. man, I find him just a little too eager to please. I know my father needs all the help he can get—he is, after all, my father—and we need someone who will not be afraid to tell him what he needs…what he *must*…hear."

A thin, consumptive-looking man wearing a cook's apron and hat appeared in the doorway, and knocked on the open door frame.

Kevin turned partly around to face him. "Yes, John?"

"Sorry to interrupt, reverend, but the oven's acting up again."

Kevin sighed. "Okay, John, I'll be right down."

John nodded, turned back toward the stairs, and disappeared.

"I'm sorry, Dick. This happens on a regular basis, I'm afraid, and I'm becoming something of an expert in oven repair out of necessity. Could we continue our talk sometime later?"

"Sure," I said as we both rose from our chairs. "Just call me at the office whenever you need me."

We shook hands, and once again it seemed the shake went on a bit longer than necessary.

"Would it be an imposition for me to ask for your home number, Dick?" Kevin asked, still maintaining the handclasp.

"With so much to be done and so little time, I might need your advice at unusual times. I promise I'll do my best not to make a pest of myself, or interfere with your personal life."

If one can think in question marks, then ????, I thought.

"No problem," I said, breaking the handshake. I took out my business card and the pen I try to always carry with me, wrote my home number on the back, and handed it to him. He looked at it carefully, as if memorizing it, then put it in his shirt pocket.

"Thanks," he said.

I followed him down the stairs and left him at the archway to the dining room. He extended his hand yet again, and we shook one more time—quickly, this time.

"Good luck with the oven," I said as he moved into the dining room and toward the kitchen.

I walked out into the street, trying to turn off the "*Ping! Ping! Ping!*" sounding in the back of my head.

CHAPTER 5

Chris had accepted the New York job at about the same time I was meeting with Kevin, so Friday night was kind of a strange one. We both felt awkward, and nervous, and neither of us knew exactly what to do or say. The whole thing reminded me oddly of a first, blind date.

Chris, I could tell, felt really guilty about having been the one to make the first—or should I say the final—move that would lead to the definite end of our relationship as lovers. We each, as we sat at the table after dinner, drinking probably too much wine, kept up the half-hearted pretense that there might be a chance of my moving to New York after he got settled, and after Rourke's campaign, but neither of us was fooling the other, or ourselves.

We decided not to make a big issue of it with our friends, or to go out of our way notify them immediately. I did suggest we have a party the Saturday before he left, and he thought that would be a good idea.

In a way, I knew, it would be harder on Chris than on me, in that I would still be able to see our friends on a regular basis, whereas he would be, at least at first, on his own. But I also realized that traditionally, couples tend to hang out with couples, and that I would become something of a fifth wheel in our circle of married friends, and that we would most likely drift apart after awhile. There were definite changes on the very near horizon for both of us.

After the wine was gone, we cleared the table, just leaving the dishes in the sink, and went into the living room. I poured us both a small glass of Cointreau, and sat beside Chris on the sofa. We didn't say much, just staring out the huge picture window at the giant oak tree directly in front of it, watching its leaves move back and forth in the light wind.

Chris reached out and took my hand. We intertwined our fingers without having to look at each other, and Chris, still staring out the window, squeezed my hand and said: "I still love you, you know."

I turned to look at him. "Yeah," I said, "I know. And I love you. And I want more than anything for you to be happy …" I'd started to say "…and find someone" but didn't. Chris stood up, still holding my hand, and pulled me to my feet.

"How about one for the road?" he asked, and I followed him into the bedroom.

We watched each other undress, like we were doing it for the first time. Chris took off his shirt and I was able to really appreciate, for the first time in a long time, what a nice body he had. His chest was covered in fine, black hair that spread from just above his nipples all the way across his pecs, and then formed a "V" pointing to his crotch. He had a slight curve to the left which had struck me as odd when we'd first gotten together, but which I hadn't even noticed in the intervening years. He sat on the bed to remove his shoes, socks, and pants, while I finished stripping, standing up.

He lay back on the bed, legs spread, and I walked over and knelt between them. I let my tongue and mouth wander from his belly button downward. After a couple of minutes, Chris scooted up on the bed and I followed; I heard him open the nightstand drawer to get out the Albolene. I straddled him on my knees, my heartbeat obvious and becoming even more demanding when he twisted the greased-up pole from tip to base. At last I backed away.

I moved back down between his legs and as I probed the target, Chris pulled my head down and kissed me.

"Remember," he whispered, as I moved forward into him.

*　　*　　*

Saturday morning we fixed our usual breakfast, and did some

casual talking about the move, and the party. There were far too many details to try to go over all at once, so we stuck to generalities. Chris would probably try to find a furnished place for a month or two until he knew what was going on and had a chance to look around for something he really wanted. He might even consider the possibility of a roommate in the interim, if such an opportunity presented itself, but he wouldn't specifically set out to look for one.

We could discuss the furniture issue later. Chris had been offered a generous moving allowance, which he planned to put aside until he knew for sure what he might need. Almost everything in our apartment was either bought jointly or hand-made. When we first got together, we'd spent lots of time at thrift shops and second hand stores, picking up things in which we saw promise, and refinishing them ourselves. We still had the sofa we'd built from a slab of plywood we'd lacquered ebony and topped with an upholstered foam pad and bolsters. Sounds ugly as sin, but it really turned out kind of nice, and was actually quite comfortable. And of course, we liked it mostly because it was ours, and we'd built it together. Chris had some favorite pieces I knew he'd probably want, and there was a lot of little stuff, and all the birthday gifts and anniversary gifts, and Christmas gifts…

Chris would leave the car—he wouldn't need it in New York, whereas I had to have some way of getting around here. I used it more than he did anyway, since he preferred taking the bus to work. Though neither of us mentioned it, it was fairly well understood that I'd offer to buy it at some point.

It's amazing how much can be communicated without actually saying much.

The day passed in 5-year routine; grocery shopping, dry cleaners, emptying ashtrays, watering the plants, doing dishes, changing the bed, picking up the living room….stuff you never, ever notice until you realize that each action is now being performed within a box of limited time. And then you're aware, and there's a sad little pang of loss and longing as you do each one.

We talked to several friends during the course of normal Saturday informal phone calls, and mentioned casually to each one that Chris had been offered a fantastic job in New York and that I would be staying here, and inviting them to the party in two weeks. Most of them, though obviously concerned and curious to know more, simply went along with our casual lead. A few asked discreet questions, which we discreetly deflected or answered as briefly and simply as possible, assuring them that this wasn't a "breakup," merely a loving separation.

As evening approached, and we sat down with our usual cocktails, Chris said:"Should I ask if you want to go out tonight?"

"Haven't we gone out almost every Saturday night for the past five years? Why shouldn't we go tonight…if you want to, that is."

"Yeah, I'd like to," Chris said.

"Then done and done."

* * *

We decided to do something special for our dinner, and went clear across town to Villa Milano, a straight place, but with the best pizza this side of…well, Milan. We both loved the place, but seldom went there simply because of the distance. This night, the distance wasn't a factor.

"So, where to now?" Chris asked as we signaled the waiter for the check and a box to carry home the few remaining slices of pizza.

"I know this might kind of surprise you," I said, "but for some reason, I feel like going back to see Judy at Bacchus' Lair."

Chris grinned. "Ah, another convert!"

"That okay with you?" I asked.

"Sure! And you can steal me one of those bunches of plastic grapes, as a souvenir."

"How about me just putting up a little memorial plaque saying 'These are Chris's'?"

"Chicken!" Chris said as the waiter returned with our doggie box.

*   *   *

We called ahead from the restaurant to try to reserve a table, and were informed that we would be first on the waiting list. We decided to risk it, anyway, and arrived at Bacchus' Lair about 20 minutes before the second show. I remembered hearing somewhere that the Dog Collar, about a block down on Arnwood, was having a weekend long anniversary party. Parking was impossible, so we drove around the block, looking for an available space and finally found one about two doors down from the Salvation's Door shelter. I was a little hesitant about leaving the car there, but the street was lined with other cars, so I thought we'd be fairly safe. I pointed the shelter out to Chris as we walked past. "Love what they've done with the place," Chris commented, noting the blocked-over windows.

When we climbed the stairs to Bacchus' Lair, we were amazed to find the place only half full. So much for being first on the waiting list. We were even able to specify a seat near the exit. (I'd checked, as we walked up to the place, and noticed for the first time that there was a narrow passageway between the bar and the building next door, just wide enough for a fire escape. Well, it was better than nothing.)

We sat down ordered drinks. "How come so quiet tonight?" I asked the cute-and-knew-it waiter.

The waiter shrugged. "Last two nights," he amended. "Everybody's been over at the Dog Collar," he said. "They're having a male stripper marathon. Which would *you* rather see? Hot sweaty naked guys or overweight drag queens?" And without waiting for an answer, he left.

"He has a point," I said to Chris.

"Maybe we can drop by there after the show," Chris said.

"Sure," I replied, reaching into my pocket for a pack of cigarettes. "Shit! I left my cigarettes at the restaurant! Where's the cigarette machine?"

"Down the back hall, near the john," Chris said. "Need some change?"

I checked my pockets. "Yeah, you got two quarters?"

Chris dug into his pocket and came up with a fistful of change. "Here," he said, then immediately hoisted up his hip to reach his wallet as he saw the waiter approaching with our drinks.

"Be right back," I said, and wove my way through the maze of mostly empty tables to the hallway leading to the john. As long as I was there, I thought I should stop in so I wouldn't be tempted later.

The cigarette machine sat in a small alcove directly next to the bathroom door, over which was a dim light. And under the dim light was a bunch of those god-awful plastic grapes. I saw they had apparently fallen off at one time and had been re-attached to the light with a piece of string. Without thinking, I reached up and yanked them off the fixture, stepping quickly back into the bathroom. I saw that they were made up of several small 'bunches' twisted together at the end. I untwisted them, and separated them into two separate clumps, which I barely managed to fit into my pants pockets. One bunch wouldn't have looked bad—sort of like the pair of socks a lot of guys are known to shove down their pants to make it look like they are really, really hung. But two such bulges were a tad obvious.

Nonetheless, I didn't have much choice so, looking as nonchalant as possible, I made my way back to our table. Chris had watched my approach with raised eyebrow.

"What the *hell*...?" he asked, as I sat down at an angle on the chair and fished out one of the bunches of "grapes".

"Here," I said. "Put this in your pocket."

When he saw what I was giving him, he pressed his lips together, and I thought he was going to cry again.

"What's wrong now?" I asked. "I thought you wanted them."

Chris made a quick swipe of his eyes with his free hand. "I did, damn it! It's just that it's so fucking sweet! You aren't making this any easier, you know." And he stuffed the "grapes" into his right pocket.

I realized he was right, and we exchanged weak little smiles.

Fortunately, at that moment the canned music came on, and the show started.

There were a couple of new performers, one of whom did a rather nice lip-synch to Bea Lillie's classic "There are Faeries at the Bottom of My Garden", and a really cute red-head whose looks far outmatched his talent synched to "Proud Mary." Tondelaya/Teddy came on and did "The Butcher's Son" as only he could do it. Spotting us, he gave us a Pearl Bailey wave and of course played the whole number right to us, drawing the stares of the other patrons. Too bad they couldn't have seen our baskets just then, I thought... they'd *really* be impressed.

And then it was time for Judy. The lights dimmed, a small spot focused on the purple curtains, and then they opened, to reveal a sad-looking Judy Garland. As usual, she paid absolutely no attention to the customers, and was apparently oblivious to the fact that there weren't all that many people there anyway. She stood a moment in silence, and then the music started and she went into "The Man that Got Away." *Jesus Christ!* I thought. *What a fucking song to sing in front of two guys who are breaking up!*

Chris and I studiously avoided looking at one another, but joined in the enthusiastic applause when the song ended. Once again I was sure I had seen the performer out of drag somewhere. Our mailman? The guy in the office down the hall from C.C.'s?

Next, she did "The Boy Next Door"—another unfortunate choice, under the circumstances. I was hoping she'd lighten up, but she ended her set with "You Made Me Love You." *Three out of three!*

As usual, a rousing ovation, and as usual no curtain call.

We sat there for awhile, sort of hoping Tondelaya/Teddy might come out to brighten things up, but he didn't. We took our time finishing our drinks, somehow reluctant to have the evening end.

"Dog Collar?" Chris asked.

"Why not?" I responded, and we got up to leave.

* * *

It had turned rather cool by the time we reached the street. We made a circle around to the car to drop off the plastic grapes and then turned toward the Dog Collar. I didn't much care for the place. It was a big, cavernous dump that boasted 4 pool tables and a downstairs "dungeon" for those into group sex. Like a lot of older buildings, it had very high ceilings, which the management had recently tried to make appear lower by stretching some sort of black mesh fabric from wall to wall.

The clientele, as the bar's name might indicate, was supposedly ultra-butch. I've got nothing at all against being butch, mind you—if it's authentic. But the Dog Collar crowd was plastic grapes butch. Still, it always drew a good crowd, and was obviously packed tonight.

We were about two doors from the entrance, when we heard a muffled "*Whoomp*" which sounded like it came from the alley behind the bar, and a moment or two later, the double front doors burst opened and a tidal wave of men washed out into the street, running. Shouts of..."*Fire!*" could be heard from inside and from those in the river of men gushing through the door. Chris and I stood frozen in mid step, then moved away from the buildings with the crowd and into the street. A wide, flat ribbon of smoke unfurled slowly out the top of the door, over the heads of those scrambling to get out.

No dictionary could ever have described the word "chaos" more vividly. Men were running, pushing, tripping over one another as they emerged, turning around to shout for friends still inside. Two or three guys fought against the tide, trying to go back in, but they couldn't buck the crowd coming out, and the smoke was getting heavy now.

The single fact of that outward-opening, double-door entrance was all that prevented a human logjam forming there, and blessedly anyone who made it as far as the door was able to escape.

In the far distance, the sound of sirens could be heard. The street was a milling mass of men; leathermen, pseudo leathermen, male strippers in g-strings and loincloths, college types, hunks, average Joes, older, younger; a cross section of the male gay community. Ironically, music still blared from inside the bar.

Small clusters of guys gathered together, some holding each other, some holding others back. Others pushed their way back and forth through the crowd, trying to locate friends. There were obviously many people hurt—most were coughing uncontrollably as they ran out, and others collapsed just outside the door and were dragged away from the entrance and carried across the street to be laid out on the sidewalk, where others huddled over them, doing what they could to help. Some just stood staring wide-eyed at the door as a few snake-tongues of orange fire began to lick out over the top of the doorway, as if tasting the air. The cacophony of sounds, however, could not hide what were too obviously screams from inside. The music had stopped.

Chris and I were totally walled in by the crowd, many still coughing and smelling of smoke, on one side of the semi-circle of onlookers. We weren't close enough to the front to be able to do anything, and we were sick with the feeling of helplessness. Still they kept coming out—guys at the front of the crowd, which was being driven back by the increasing heat and billowing smoke, would rush forward to grab anyone who made it through the doors and lead them to safety, or run interference to prevent others from trying to reenter the building to save friends or lovers.

We stood there, pressed against those crowded around us, and looked around to see if there was anyone we knew. Chris stood on tip-toe, trying to see over the heads of those directly around us. Fewer were coming out, now. One guy—probably one of the strippers—stumbled through the doorway, totally naked, obviously badly burned, his hair smoldering. He appeared slowly, back-lit by an angry pulsating orange, and leaned against the door frame as though it were a part of his number. Then he pushed himself forward, made it just outside the door, and toppled like a fallen tree onto the sidewalk before those dashing in to help him could reach him. They picked him up and carried across the street, the crowd parting to allow them through. And an instant later, a form appeared, from the other side of the doorway, crawling on all fours, his shirt on fire. He was grabbed and pulled forward by several guys who slapped at his shirt with their hands to put out the fire. They got him to his feet, but he looked frantically around at the crowd, then broke away and ran back toward the door, from which no one else was emerging. Two of those who'd helped him ran after him and grabbed him just before he reached the door, which was by this time engulfed in flame. They dragged him backward as he fought to break free, straining forward and yelling something we could not make out over the incredible din. There were no more screams coming from inside the bar; just the triumphant roar of the flames.

The first squad car came racing down the street, siren wailing, lights flashing, horn blasting, followed by no fewer than three fire trucks, with the lights of others closing in from both directions. The crowd scattered before them.

And over all the sirens, and the yells, and the dull thrum of the fire, which was now pouring out of the door and had broken through the roof, I heard a voice:

"*Dick! Dick!*" I looked around and Chris pointed to the guy whose shirt had been on fire, still being held by his rescuers. It was Bob Allen.

Ambulances were beginning to arrive as the firemen rolled out their hoses and the police...several squads of them by this time, began moving the crowd back to allow the arriving ambulances to get through.

We shouldered our way through the mass of guys to Bob. He had blood running down his left temple from a gash somewhere just above the hairline. But his face! I hope I never see another expression on anyone's face like I saw on Bob's. The two guys holding him, seeing that we knew him, reluctantly released him. He grabbed us both, one with each hand, and his knees started to buckle. We grabbed him and held him up between us.

He tightened his grip on our arms. "You've got to help me go back in!" he pleaded, and suddenly my head jerked up to meet Chris's eyes, which mirrored my own shock in realizing why.

"Ramón!" Bob said, pointing to the inferno. "Ramón's still in there!"

CHAPTER 6

Ramón, we later learned, was one of twenty-three men who never made it out of the Dog Collar. Another six died later in the hospitals—one from burns and five from smoke inhalation. Apparently whatever the ceiling mesh was made from had proven to be fatally toxic when burned in the confines of a closed space.

Despite Bob's dazed insistence that he stay at the fire scene until Ramón was found, his arms and back were clearly burned and we all but dragged him to one of the many ambulances shuttling back and forth to hospitals. I recognized one of the paramedics who helped Bob into the ambulance, and was told he'd be taken to St. Anthony's. We made our way back to the car through a light fog of drifting smoke, without looking back and rode in dazed silence to the hospital to wait for word on Bob.

The waiting room was already filled with friends and families of the burned and injured, and more were coming in. The number of injured taxed the hospital's bed availability beyond its capacity, and those less badly injured were merely treated and released. Luckily Bob was one of them. His burns, apparently less severe than they'd appeared to us, were treated and bandaged, the cut on his head stitched up, and he was released to us with instructions to return immediately if there were any complications, or in two days if there were not.

It was close to four a.m. by the time we drove home, again in complete silence. Bob sat in the back seat with Chris, staring straight ahead.

We did not even consider the possibility of his returning to his own apartment, and took him directly to ours, leading him into the guest room. I'm not sure he even knew where he was, let alone cared. We carefully helped him out of what remained of his clothes, and guided him into bed, on his stomach.

Neither Chris nor I slept much that night, thinking of Bob, of Ramón, and of all those others—and how, had we been a few minutes earlier getting to the bar or had the fire started a few minutes later, we may well have been standing with Bob and Ramón, watching the strippers strut their stuff on the makeshift stage at the far back of the bar.

We got up at 7:30, unable to even pretend to sleep any longer. Chris went into the kitchen to make coffee, and I went to the guest room and quietly opened the door a crack, to check on Bob. He was sitting on the edge of the bed, staring at the floor. I knocked softly, and then entered.

"Chris has the coffee on," I said, having no idea of what else to say.

Bob looked up and said "Thanks."

"We've got a couple extra robes, if you'd like one," I volunteered. "And later if you want to give me the keys to your place. I can go up and get you some clothes."

"Ramón has them," Bob said, offhandedly. "He drove last night, and he kept the keys."

Shit! What can anyone possibly do or say in a situation like that?

"Well," I said, "we'll figure something out after a while. There's no rush."

Bob merely nodded and I went quickly to the bathroom to get Bob Chris's spare robe. Bob was coming out of the door when I returned.

"Can I use your phone?" he asked.

"Sure," I said, unsure of exactly who he wanted to call. Ramón's folks, maybe—if he knew their number.

"I've got to call…" he hesitated…"*somebody* to find out if they've found Ramón."

"Well, come on in and sit down first. We'll have some coffee. Can I get you some aspirin or something?" I asked, concerned about the physical pain he must be in.

Bob shook his head. "I'll be fine," he said.

We sat in the living room and had coffee in almost complete silence. Chris asked if Bob felt like eating anything, and he shook his head.

"Chris," I said, "didn't I see Jason Young last night?" Jason was, I was sure, one of the firemen on the scene. His lover, Arnie, was on Chris' bowling team.

"Yeah, I think you're right. Kind of hard to tell in all the confusion."

"Do you happen to have their phone number?" I asked, casually. I knew that it was very unlikely that Bob—who was in no condition to be making phone calls in any case—would be able to find out any pertinent information, other than where the bodies had been taken. I knew that Jason probably hadn't slept much last night either, if at all, and he was almost definitely still on his shift. But I wanted to give it a try anyway, to help Bob start on some sense of closure. I could not begin to imagine the mental agony he must be going through, and I was selfishly glad I couldn't.

Chris got up to get us some more coffee. "I'm sure I've got the number somewhere," he said. "I'll go check."

Bob and I sat there in silence, me feeling painfully awkward in not being able to do something to help, and Bob lost in his own world.

After a moment, Bob said, without looking at me. "I left him there. He depended on me, and I left him there."

"Oh, God, Bob, no...no you didn't," I said. "It wasn't your fault."

Chris had come back with the coffee, but stopped short, pot in hand, not wanting to interrupt.

"Whenever we'd go into a crowded bar," Bob said, his voice almost conversational, "I'd always go first to lead the way, and Ramón would hook his hand through the back of my belt so we wouldn't get separated."

Chris still stood there, neither he nor I daring to move, totally focused on Bob.

"We were in the back, near the stage," Bob said. "Ramón

was leaning up against the end of the bar. The place was packed solid, and the strippers were making a fortune, with guys shoving bills into their g-strings. The music was too loud, as always. We didn't even know anything was wrong, at first, until a couple guys pointed down the hallway leading to the back door and the stairway to the dungeon, and started yelling 'Fire'!

"And then everything happened so damned fast! Everyone started backing away, at first, and then fire was running in little waves across the ceiling of the hallway and out into the main room, and the place panicked! The guys in the dungeon never had a chance!

"Ramón and I looked at each other, and I grabbed his hand and started pulling him toward the front door. God! There were so many people! Pushing and shouting, with the fire slithering across the ceiling over our heads. I was *sure* I could feel him holding onto the back of my belt, but when I got about halfway to the front, I looked back for Ramón, and he wasn't there. Just guys...so many guys. And the fire had crept around the corner of the hallway and was moving across the back wall, toward the stage. I looked up and I couldn't see the flames on the ceiling because the smoke was there, hiding it, and getting thicker and moving down towards our heads. Little bits of burning party decorations and God knows what were falling on us.

"I yelled for Ramón, but he couldn't have heard me in all that racket. And the damned music was still blaring away like nothing was wrong! I turned around and tried to go back to where we'd been standing, but I just kept getting carried forward by the crowd. I tried to at least work my way over to the bar. I thought if I could get behind the bar, I could go almost the entire length of the place without having to fight my way there. .And then I looked up, and one of the supports on one of those big fluorescent light fixtures snapped off at one end and the rest of the fixture came swinging down from the ceiling. I tried to duck but it got me right on the side of the head. I woke up on the floor right at the front end of the bar. When I came to, I saw that there was a solid ceiling of thick, pitch black smoke that came to within three feet of the floor, and was moving lower. I could hear the liquor bottles on the back bar exploding from the heat, and I started crawling toward the door, to keep as much below the smoke as I could. I couldn't see anyone else around me, so I was sure Ramón had made it out. But then when I got outside and he wasn't right there, waiting for me, I knew he hadn't, and I had to go back in and find him. I *had* to!"

He looked, for the first time, up at Chris, and then over at me.

"I left him in there," he said. "I…left…,", and his voice broke into a long, terrible wail and he began to lean forward like a crumbling wall. I reached over and grabbed him, forgetting about his burned arms and back, and hugged him to me. "*It's not your fault,*" I kept repeating "*It's not your fault*" as he muffled his wail in the cloth of my robe. Chris hadn't moved, but he was visibly shaking and biting his lip as the tears ran down his face. He managed to set the pot down and came over to sit on Bob's other side, and put his arms around us both.

*   *   *

Chris had found Arnie and Jason's number, and while Bob went with Chris into the bedroom to find him a pair of pants and a loose-fitting shirt, I saw that it was almost 10 o'clock, and the chance of waking either Arnie or Jason, if he weren't still on duty, were remote. Going to the kitchen phone, I dialed the number. I did not recognize the voice, but took a chance that it would most probably be Arnie, I said: "Arnie? This is Dick Hardesty— Chris's other half."

"Hi, Dick," he said, his voice tired. "What can I do for you?"

"You heard about the Dog Collar, of course," I said.

"It's all over the news," Arnie said, "…local *and* national. God, what a waste!"

"Chris and I were there," I said, hastening to add "but weren't inside when it started. There aren't any words…. But I thought I saw Jason there, on one of the units. I assume he's still on shift?"

"Yeah," Arnie said. "But he gets off at noon. I talked to him earlier and he sounded really down; he didn't say so because he was calling from work, but I suspect he knew a couple of the guys who didn't make it. I hope I didn't know any of them." There was a pause, then a tentative "Why did you want to talk to him, Dick? I really don't think he's going to be in the mood for a lot of questions about the fire."

"No, Arnie, I understand. And I wouldn't have called at all if it weren't really important. You know Bob Allen, don't you? He owned the Ebony Room?"

"Sure. We used to go…" he paused. "Oh, God, Dick, you don't mean he was…."

"He wasn't, but his lover Ramón was," I said. "We've got Bob here at our place."

"Christ, I'm sorry, Dick. Please tell him how sorry we are."

"I will, Arnie, thanks. But they were together in the bar when the fire started, and they got separated, and Bob is tearing himself apart with guilt. He *really* needs help on this, Arnie. If he could just find out exactly what happened to Ramón, at least it will help him deal with it. The regular information channels will be blocked solid for God knows how long. I figured that since Jason was there, he might know something… anything… that could help."

Arnie was quiet for a moment and said "I guess you haven't been watching the news reports on the fire."

"Most definitely not," I said. "Not with Bob here."

"Yeah; of course not.," Arnie said. "But I probably should prepare you: according to the reports, most of the bodies were burned beyond recognition. It'll be days before positive identification can be made."

"Shit!," I said. I was afraid that might be the case. "But some have already been identified?"

"I gather. But rather than speculate, Dick, why don't I talk to Jason as soon as he gets home, and see if he has any informa-tion at all that could help. Okay?"

"Thanks, Arnie," I said. "I know it will mean a *lot* to Bob."

There was a moment's pause, and I was just about to say "goodbye" when Arnie said: "You know, Dick, I try not to think about it, but every time I hear there's a big fire somewhere, and Jason is on duty, I just...well, I can't imagine how losing him would be. Again, please tell Bob we're thinking of him."

"I will, Arnie. Again, thanks, and I'll hope to hear from Jason. So long."

Arnie said "Bye", and hung up.

* * *

I called the building supervisor, explaining that Bob had been in an accident and lost his keys. The supervisor said he thought he had an extra set, and that if he found them he would bring them up to our apartment. About 20 minutes later, the supervisor rang our bell.

"There's a $25 fee for lost keys," he said. "Will he be needing the mailbox key, too? That'll be another $10."

I took the keys out of his hand, told him we'd get back to him, and closed the door.

Chris insisted that we had to eat something, and Bob reluctantly agreed, though he said he wasn't even remotely hungry. We went into the kitchen, and Chris rummaged through the refrigerator, pulling out some lunch meat, butter, mayonnaise, mustard, lettuce, and some macaroni salad he'd made a day or so before. "How about a glass of milk, Bob?" he asked. "Or more coffee?"

"A little milk's okay," Bob said. And Chris brought out the milk, and got the bread, and some silverware, and a few small plates, and.... "I think this'll do it for now, Chris," I said, and gave him a little smile.

"Sure," he said, and came to join us at the table.

We ate slowly, and though none of us had eaten in 15 hours or more, none of us was really hungry.

The phone rang, and Chris got up to answer it. He held it

out to me. "It's Jason," he said. "I think he should talk to you."

"I think I'll take it in the living room," I said, and got up from the table.

*   *   *

"Chris, you and Bob want to come in the living room?" I called, as I hung up the phone. Chris had apparently told Bob the reason I'd called Arnie and Jason in the first place, and anxiety showed clearly on both their faces. Chris hovered over Bob until he'd seated himself on the couch.

"They found Ramón?" Bob asked.

I nodded. "Jason recognized him when they brought him out," I said. "He and Arnie used to come into the Ebony Room." Bob sat very still, listening. I was trying to pick words that would hurt the least, but realized that was impossible, so I just forged ahead.

"He didn't die from the fire," I began, hoping that knowledge might give him even an atom's worth of comfort. "He hardly had a mark on him, Jason said. Something had fallen over him that protected him from the flames. They believe it was the smoke that was responsible for many of…why a lot of the guys on the main floor didn't make it out. It was extremely toxic, probably from that mesh dropped ceiling." Bob still hadn't moved, just sat there with his eyes downcast.

"Jason says it's a very quick way to go;" I said. "Just a couple of breaths, actually. And Jason knows what he's talking about. He's almost certain Ramón didn't suffer."

Bob looked up at me, his eyes red, but his voice under control: "Thanks, Dick." He turned to Chris: "Thanks, Chris."

What I didn't tell Bob—what I could not bring myself to tell him and prayed he would never find out—was that they found Ramón behind the bar, probably only 10 feet away from where Bob fell, trying to find him.

CHAPTER 7

Neither Chris nor I went in to work on Monday Neither of us wanted to leave Bob alone, and there was a lot to be done—notifying Ramón's family in Puerto Rico, making whatever arrangements they might request, getting Bob's car out of the impound lot where it had been taken—with many other cars, whose owners would not be coming back to them. I called the office to say I would not be in, but I gave no reason and no one called to demand one.

We got up early again, and found Bob already up and in the living room, watching the news. The fire was still the major story, and though the TV crews had not arrived until well after the main part of the fire was extinguished, the sight of the now empty street, a jumble of debris and fire hoses snaking around the remaining fire trucks, the front of the gutted building with wisps of smoke still rising from it and, worst of all, a quick, almost sidelong shot of a long line of blanketed forms stretched out on the sidewalk across the street were all too painful reminders of the crowd, and the noise, and the knowledge of what had happened.

It was the worst fire in the city's history, and it not only plunged the gay community into mourning, but rallied it as nothing had done before. Much of the straight community responded as well. Funds were set up to help pay medical expenses for the injured, and to help bury the dead. Newspapers which had relegated the six previous gay bar fires to one-or-two paragraph notices buried deep in the bowels of the paper, surrounded by ads for blenders and pantyhose, now belatedly decried the fact that there was an arsonist loose in the city and demanded that something be done to catch him. Of course, in the papers' defense, it could be pointed out that no one had died in the previous fires.

Still, the fire and the senseless deaths had apparently made a lot of heterosexuals wake up to the possibility that a homosexual's life just might have value, too.

The Sunday supplement had come out with the story on the chief and his family as its lead article, but the fire had made it totally irrelevant.

* * *

By Monday night, most of what had to be done had been done. There were several calls to Ramón's parents—Chris and I alternated in them. Bob had wanted to tell them himself, but realized he wouldn't be able to; Ramón had not been out to his family. But they had heard of the fire, of course, and it probably didn't require too much to figure out the obvious. They requested that his body be sent to Puerto Rico for burial, and Bob agreed. We contacted two funeral homes we knew to be owned or operated by gays, but they were already swamped, and we had to call several others before we found one which could make the arrangements.

When I drove down to the morgue to see about picking up Ramón's personal items and Bob's keys, I was told that someone would have to make positive identification of the body. I couldn't put Bob through that so I told them I would do it. I was taken into a small room with a curtained window, and a moment later the curtain was opened to show an attendant standing beside a sheet-covered form on a gurney. I forced myself to turn my emotions off, and nodded. The attendant pulled back the sheet to reveal Ramón's face, looking as though he were asleep. I'd never seen Ramón asleep. I never would. I just nodded again, and the attendant covered Ramón's face and closed the curtains.

Later in the afternoon Chris, Bob, and I drove down to the impound lot to retrieve Bob's car, which Chris drove back to the apartment.

While I was at the morgue, Chris and Bob had gone up to

Bob's apartment, where they found the answering machine filled with messages from Bob's and Ramón's friends, who'd either somehow heard through the grapevine or seen Ramón's name in the only newspaper which had printed a list of the dead.

Chris got carry-out for dinner, and we sat around the apartment talking of just about anything but the fire.

Finally, Bob said: "I think it's time I headed upstairs to my place."

Chris said "Are you sure? You're more than welcome to stay here as long as you want," and I nodded in agreement.

Bob smiled for the first time since the fire—a small smile, but a smile nonetheless —and said: "You know I can never repay you two for what you've done, but I have to start getting on with my life sometime, and it might as well be now."

"Okay, then," I said, "but promise you'll call if there's anything you need; and if you change your mind about spending the night here...."

Bob got up from the sofa. "I'll be fine," he said. "Really." Chris and I got up and followed him to the door. He started to extend his hand to Chris, and then changed his mind and hugged him, tight. "I owe you," he said. Then it was my turn. When he released the hug, he backed up a bit and looked me in the eye. "Thanks," he said, and then turned, opened the door, and went out into the hallway.

*   *   *

The chief's candidacy-announcing press conference had been set up weeks in advance for what turned out to be the Tuesday following the fire. One of the larger meeting rooms of the Convention Center had been reserved, and the conference had been scheduled for precisely 4:30 p.m. to maximize coverage on the evening news. Every detail of the event had been painfully staged to present the chief in the best possible light, down to the discussion of whether or not he should wear his uniform (yes, since few people would recognize him without it) and his hat (no, because even with carefully placed lighting there was the chance that the brim might cast a shadow which would give him an even more sinister look than he had without it). The fundamental objective was to minimize any possible chance for spontaneity. Spontaneity was not the chief's strong suite, and everyone except possibly the chief himself knew it.

But from the minute the body count began to come in from the Dog Collar, everything went up for grabs. A few of the chief's advisers suggested that in the wake of the fire, with the funerals and burials of the dead beginning Tuesday, the chief should postpone the press conference—or at least his candidacy announcement—but the chief wasn't going to let a few dead faggots stand in the way of his big moment, and the conference schedule remained unchanged. It was obvious, even to C.C. if not to the chief, that the reporters were going to be far more interested in what was being done about the fire than in the chief's throwing his hat into the political ring. C.C. and the chief's political honchos gathered early Sunday morning at the chief's City Hall office—he dared not be anywhere else, under the circumstances—and his early morning arrival, striding stern-faced (he actually had no other) through pre-notified crowds of reporters and camera crews from around the state and the country, gave strong evidence that he was in control of the situation. C.C. and the others entered quietly through side and rear doors.

And so while the chief's seconds in command spent Sunday and much of Monday actually, if reluctantly, dealing with the Dog Collar fire, the chief, except for a few carefully selected photo-ops (the chief solemnly behind his desk, surrounded by his deeply concerned top aids, gravely discussing the status of the investigation; the chief inspecting the gutted interior of Dog Collar with the fire chief) spent the bulk of his time being carefully rehearsed on exact responses to every conceivable question he might be faced with come Tuesday's press conference.

*   *   *

Tuesday morning, I reluctantly returned to work, and to bedlam About halfway through the morning, having carefully examined and boxed the press kits and made several phone calls to verify the readiness of the meeting room for the press conference, I found, buried on my desk, two phone messages from Kevin: one dated Monday, the second about half an hour before I'd gotten to work.

Curious, I called the number on the slips.

"Salvation's Door Shelter." I didn't recognize the voice.

"May I speak to Ke...to Reverend...Rourke, please?"

"Just a second." I heard the phone being put down and the sound of receding footsteps, then silence for a good minute and a half, and finally the sound of footsteps again...approaching, this time...and the receiver being lifted.

"Reverend Rourke."

"Kevin," I said: "it's Dick Hardesty."

"Oh, yes! I'm glad you called. I tried to reach you yesterday, but they said you were gone for the day. I hope you weren't ill."

"No," I said, giving no further explanation. "Can I help you with anything?"

"Well, I wanted to let you know that I'd spoken Saturday with my father regarding our idea for the Shelter fund raiser, and he did not seem adverse to the idea. He said he would have to pass it by his political advisers first, of course."

Damn! Any political adviser worth his salt would see the trip-wire on that little booby trap. Still, it's the kind of logical proposal that would be a little hard to reject out of hand.

"That's fine," I said. "Let me know what he decides, and we can get started on it as soon as he agrees."

There was a slight pause, and then: "There were a few other things I thought we might talk over, if you have the time," Kevin said. "I know today is a very busy one for all of us, but I was wondering if we might meet for lunch."

Ping! Ping! Ping!

I should have declined, of course, but what the hell? I needed to get my mind off the fire, and Kevin was becoming more and more an intriguing puzzle. I can never resist trying to solve puzzles. And C.C. couldn't possibly object. He's the one who'd told me that whatever Kevin wanted, Kevin was supposed to get.

"Sure," I said. "What time?"

"It might be cutting things a little close, but would one o'clock be all right? We serve lunch here between 11:30 and 12:30. I can set aside a couple lunches, if you wouldn't mind sharing what we serve our flock?"

"Not at all," I said. "And one o'clock is fine. I'll see you then." And I hung up.

My phone buzzed just as I set the receiver back on the cradle.

"Hardesty. I want to see you in my office," and there was a click at the other end of the line. *Gee, I wonder who that might have been?* I said to myself, as I got up and headed toward C.C.'s office.

I knocked and, as was part of his little game, there was silence from inside until I knocked again. "Come," C.C.'s imperious voice commanded.

I walked to his desk, not expecting to be asked to sit. I wasn't.

"You'll be at the Center no later than 2:30 to be damned sure everything's set up."

I'd been working on exactly that ever since C.C. first took on the chief as a project—and assigned most of the actual work to me.

"Everything's ready to go, Mr. Carlson," I said.

"Well for your sake I hope to hell you're right. Any snafu's and it'll be *your* ass in the wringer." There was a pause while he furrowed his brows, trying to think of something I might have overlooked. "Did you double check with the electricians to see that there's plenty of power for the TV crews, if they need it?"

"Yes."

"And coffee? Gotta make sure the coffee's there for the reporters while they're waiting. And none of those Styrofoam cups, you hear?"

"Yes" I said. C.C. knew damned good and well the Center routinely handled dozens of events in the course of any given month, and knew what they were doing. "Oh," I added, "and I should mention that Kevin has asked me to stop by the shelter at one o'clock. He has some things he wants to talk over." Actually, I didn't need to mention it at all, but I wanted to remind old C.C. that I was developing a pretty strong ally in the Rourke camp, lest he foolishly decide to push me a little too far.

"Well, then, don't just stand around here—you've got work to do. Go do it."

I didn't wait for the dismissive wave, but merely turned and left his office, closing the door behind me.

*   *   *

Driving down 16th, I deliberately kept myself from looking to my left as I passed Arnwood. I didn't want to risk catching any glimpse of the police barricades still in front of the Dog Collar. I just kept seeing Ramón sitting on the floor with his back resting between Bob's legs, talking and laughing and alive.

There were quite a few street people milling around in the immediate vicinity of Salvation's Door when I arrived at about 10 'til 1. Not too many cars on the street, so I parked directly across from the door, locked the car, and went in.

Several people were still in the dining room, and I saw Kevin standing by the door to the kitchen, talking with one of the workers. I stood there until I caught his eye. He smiled and motioned that I should go on up to his office, which I did. I was aware of the faint smell of smoke.

I stood behind Kevin's desk, idly looking at the notices on the bulletin board, until I heard him climbing the stairs. He entered the room with a tray holding two bowls of soup, a couple sandwiches, spoons wrapped in paper napkins, and two small cartons of milk. He looked at the desk, trying to figure out where to set the tray down, and then motioned with his head to a space behind the open door. "There's a TV tray there, I think. If you don't mind, we could probably share it."

"Fine," I said, moving to get the tray and set it up in front of his desk. He set the tray down and we cleared off the two wooden chairs and set them in the same places as my first visit.

"I try to keep these chairs clear," he said, "but they just keep getting filled up."

We sat down, and I waited in rather awkward silence as Kevin lowered his head in prayer. "Amen," I heard him say, and he opened his eyes and smiled at me. It struck me that he *did* have a sexy smile. "Let's eat," he said.

The soup, minestrone, was really excellent, and I told him so. He seemed pleased.

"We really do do the best we can with what we have," he said.

The sandwiches appeared to be ham salad, and I nodded in approval as I took my first bite. We ate in silence for a few moments before I said: "I've got to be at the Center in just a little while to make sure everything's set up for the conference," I said, "so perhaps we could…."

"Of course," Kevin said. "As you know, my father will be addressing the State Association of Police Chiefs' annual meeting on the 26th—that's two weeks from this coming Saturday. It can be a very effective forum for him, and if we can provide some solid media coverage, it will offer a good opportunity for getting his message out to the public."

I finished my sandwich and opened the carton of milk as he spoke.

"Mr. Carlson will be there, of course," Kevin said, finishing his own sandwich and using the paper napkin to wipe a crumb from one corner of his mouth, "and apparently you'll be accompanying him."

This was news to me, but….

"As you know," Kevin continued, "this will be a very expensive campaign, and money is tight…"

I'm afraid my eyes opened a bit wide on that one, but I said nothing, and Kevin didn't seem to notice.

"...so we have to do a bit of belt-tightening on travel expenses. Sue-Lynn and the baby won't be able to come with us, I'm afraid, and so I was wondering if you would consider it too much of an imposition if we were to share a hotel room to cut down expenses."

No *Ping! Ping! Ping!* : more like *Clang! Clang! Clang!* Something sure as hell was going on here, and I still didn't know exactly what.

"Uh..." I said, then figured *What the Hell?* and dove in. "That would be fine."

"Good," he said and, finishing his milk, he reached forward to lift the TV tray from between us and move it to one side. "By the way, I hope the smell of smoke doesn't bother you I'm afraid it's a result of that...fire. You heard about it, of course."

"Yes," I said. "I heard."

Kevin sat once again leaning slightly forward, with his elbows on the arms of his chair and his hands lightly folded.

"It was a real tragedy," Kevin said, shaking his head. "All those men...." He moved back slowly in his chair, one arm now laying the length of the chair arm, fingers curled lightly over the edge, the other on his leg. He sighed: "Of course, the Good Book does say: 'The wages of sin...'"

I couldn't help myself: my head snapped up and I stared at him in disbelief. He caught my eyes, and dropped his head slightly, adding quickly "...but of course we are all God's children."

I looked down at his lap, and his cupped hand had moved up his leg and was slowly sweeping across his crotch, his fingers spreading open.

Jesus Christ! Is this guy groping himself?

I got up out of my chair so fast it seemed to startle him. He acted as though he had no idea at all of what he had been doing!

"I'd really better get going over to the Center," I said. "There's a lot to be done yet. Thanks for lunch."

Kevin got up and moved the TV tray further out of the way. "Of course," he said."I'll see you at the press conference, then," he said, smiling and extending his hand. I took it, and it was very warm, and very firm, and just slightly damp.

*   *   *

The chief's reputation having preceded him throughout the state, and indeed the nation, guaranteed a good-sized turnout for his announcement. His take-no-prisoners /hang-'em-at-the-airport approach to law enforcement had pretty much polarized people as few others, in or out of government, have done or could do. The darling of the conservatives and the antichrist to liberals, the fact was that while nearly everyone had a strong opinion on *what* the chief was, almost no one had even the foggiest idea of *who* he was. I personally had reached the conclusion that there was the uniform and all it represented, and there was the man. And that each was the other.

At precisely 4:30 p.m., the chief's entourage filed in to the room, forming a precise, pre-arranged tableau that would have been the envy of any military drill team. The family was there, all perfectly scrubbed and coifed, beaming with pride and looking like a Christmas card portrait photo. Kevin was there, left arm (to display his wedding ring and therefore his family-man worthiness) wrapped lovingly around Sue-Lynn who, as always, cradled little Sean at exactly the most photogenic angle. The other children were lined up in descending order of importance in front of Mrs. Rourke, whom I hadn't even noticed on my first glance. On either side of the raised platform stood various pillars of the community, and a smattering of local and state bigwigs. And closest to the podium in the gaggle of dignitaries on the right-hand side of the stage, and leading the applause as the chief strode into the room, stood a proud Carlton Carlson.

The chief stepped to the podium, laid several large sheets of paper on it, and began:

"Before I make the announcement for which this news conference was called," he said, his voice stentorian in its solemnity, "I would like to say a brief word in acknowledgment of the recent fatal fire which struck our community, and to personally convey my own and my family's deepest heartfelt condolences to the mothers and fathers, the sisters and brothers, the grandparents and other relatives of those who died."

That's it? That's IT?? I thought for a second there I was going to lose it. *You FUCKING BASTARD!!!* I wanted to scream: *What about THEM? What about their lovers and their friends? What about the entire gay community? Why don't you just go up and spit on their coffins?*

The chief, of course, was as oblivious to my rage as he was to anything else which did not serve his own purposes. After only a momentary pause, he continued.

"While I'm sure you all have questions regarding the progress of the case, I can only assure you that we are at a critical stage in the investigation, and are devoting all the efforts of both the fire and police departments to find and prosecute those responsible for this act. But since it is an ongoing investigation, I will be making no further comments at this time."

There was a muted murmur from the crowd, which the Chief silenced by an authoritarian raising of one hand.

"It is" he said, launching into his speech, "exactly this type of rampant lawlessness which underscores the urgency of providing those charged with protecting our citizens the tools and support they must have to do their job properly and thoroughly. We must once and for all say to the criminals who roam our streets with impunity: Enough!"

He then laid out a detailed and carefully worded litany of everything that was wrong with the current governor and his policies—which was to say, *everything.* I had to hand it to his trainers; his message was a puff pastry of political correctness, but the filling was pure storm-trooper.

He rambled on for what seemed like an eternity, and I totally tuned out until at last I dimly heard: "And it is to this end that I am today announcing my candidacy for governor of this great state!"

There was a burst of enthusiastic applause from the assembly on the stage. Flashbulbs strobed the room, and before the gathered reporters had a chance to start shouting their questions, C.C. shot me a stern glance from across the room and I cued the guy with the sound equipment. The happy strains of "Yankee Doodle" filled the air. C.C. had originally considered "Hail to the Chief" but was talked out of it. He also wanted balloons to drop down from the ceiling, but it would have been too short a drop to be practical.

As if on cue—which in fact it was—the chief's family moved forward to embrace him warmly. It did not escape me that a few of the younger children appeared to be totally confused by this unfamiliar outpouring of familial love.

The two bands of supporters simultaneously moved in from both sides of the stage for congratulatory photo-op handshakes and back-pats, and I suddenly realized that the chief actually thought that he could use this orchestrated outburst of wild enthusiasm—which was limited entirely to the stage—as a smoke screen to signal that the "press conference" was over.

Making sure that C.C. wasn't looking, I gave the sound man a signal to fade out the music. The moment it died, the reporters began jostling forward, shouting questions in an attempt to be heard over the other shouted questions. The chief and C.C. looked a bit startled, and C.C. glared at me, but I merely looked at him innocently as if to say "What?".

Reluctantly, the chief returned to the podium as the rest of the throng on stage moved back, as if distancing themselves from the onslaught of questions.

"Chief!" the reporter closest to the stage shouted, "The Dog Collar was a gay bar, and all 29 victims were assumedly gay men. Is your investigation centering on known hate groups?"

The chief had obviously been prepared for that one. "As I stated in my opening remarks," he said, both hands gripping the edges of the podium, "this is an ongoing investigation in a crucial stage of development; and I could not at this point even speculate on the motivation behind the blaze." I'm sure that is all he was supposed to say, but being the chief he had to add a little something of his own " Hate groups, a jealous boyfriend…I simply cannot speculate."

A jealous boyfriend? Did he SAY that??? Did he actually SAY that??? I turned, almost knocking over the chair behind me in my hurry to leave the room. I didn't know whether to yell or cry, but I did neither and instead went to the bathroom to splash cold water on my face and pull myself together.

I can't do this, I told the obviously shaken me in the mirror. *I can't put up with this shit one single minute longer!*

"*Yeah, you can,*" the me in the mirror replied. "*You have to. You're the only one who has any idea of what's going on on the inside of that pocket-Hitler's little clique. And if you blow it by making it obvious you're gay, who'll be there to try and stop him?*"

He was right. I wanted a cigarette, but knew I'd probably been gone too long already, so I returned to the conference room.

I don't know what the questioning had been like while I was gone, but it appeared that the chief was holding his own, though I could tell from the way he was clutching the edges of the podium and the narrowing of his eyes that he was mentally making an 'enemies list' of reporters for future reference.

At last it was over. The chief thanked everyone for coming and reminded them that his door was always open to the press. *Yeah,* I thought, *like the door's always open to the bank vault.* He turned, awkwardly hugged his wife, put out his hand to Mary, his youngest, who took it with ill-concealed trepidation, and together the family left the stage, followed by the remainder of the party. The reporters gathered up their gear and left, leaving me to clear up the mess.

CHAPTER 8

The next week and a half went by fast—way too fast. At this rate, I figured, I'd be 97 years old before I knew it.

Bob and a few close friends—Chris and I were touched to be asked to be among them—had a simple memorial service for Ramón at the local M.C.C. on Thursday night, and his body was sent to his parents on Friday for burial. Bob was holding up very well, under the circumstances, but there was a definite change in him.

On Saturday, the one-week anniversary of the fire, there was a huge impromptu silent memorial for all the victims held on the street in front of the Dog Collar. Thousands of gays, lesbians, and straights, alerted only by word of mouth, gathered in silence at sundown to lay flowers in front of the yellow barricades outside the gutted bar, and to pay the dead the respect their Chief of Police and now aspiring gubernatorial candidate had refused them. In an act of defiance by the community, no police permits were obtained in advance even though the crowd filled the street and completely blocked traffic. While the police were in evidence, it seemed mostly—and unnecessarily—to keep anyone from entering the cordoned-off area. Nothing was done to interfere with the memorial. Not even the chief would have been stupid enough to try.

When we heard that Bob planned on attending the service, we insisted that he go with us, and we kept a close watch on him. But he just stood with everyone else, staring into what remained of the open door of the Dog Collar. There were many tears in the crowd, but none from Bob.

The "ongoing investigation" into the fire remained ongoing. I had spoken to Tom, briefly on the phone. He couldn't say much over the phone, of course, but I got the impression the arson squad, at least, was sincerely doing their best to piece the puzzle together. I had several questions I wanted to ask him but they would have to wait. We tentatively planned to meet at the memorial on Saturday, but there were so many people there, we missed each other. I called him again the following Monday and left a message on his machine.

On Thursday, the newspapers and TV stations headlined the story that an arrest had been made in the Dog Collar fire case: the bar's owner, for "criminal endangerment" of his patrons by exceeding occupancy limits, by putting up the toxic mesh to begin with, and for not providing more than one exit from the basement, where most of the victims had died.

As to the arrest of the actual arsonist...

Our plans for Chris' going away party had changed drastically, of course. We still wanted to have all our friends over for one last time, but the emphasis had definitely shifted from the status of a "party" to a "gathering." Chris had bought his tickets, and would be leaving on the morning of the 25th, the day I was to head up to the police chiefs' meeting.

My days at work were hectic, as C.C. got out his drums and whips to beat us into rowing the chief's barge ever faster. Endless press releases, lengthy phone calls to newspapers throughout the state offering fill-in-the-dots-with-local-color stories. Requests for interviews with the chief were declined on the grounds of his deep involvement in the fire investigation. Personal appearances were kept to an absolute minimum with the same excuse, and the fire had in fact given the chief a perfect alibi for not having to run the risk of having to face real people. Stories were "leaked" by the chief's insiders as to how profoundly he regretted not being able to be out there among the voters, but that his commitment to his duties as Chief of Police, and his protection of the citizens of his home city, had to take precedence over politics. Made him seem noble as all shit.

Only a few contacts with Kevin; all by phone. He was spending much of his time making quick trips around the state, speaking before church groups and various conservative organizations on his father's behalf, trumpeting the message of the chief's deep concern for the restoration of law, order, and moral values. Sue-Lynn and the baby accompanied him whenever possible, of course, and anyone seeing them together would have little doubt that they did in truth epitomize everything America—and therefore the chief— stood for.

The bars were suffering huge financial losses, their business down by as much as 80 percent. Even the lesbian bars were affected, though none of them had ever been firebombed. Understandably, the Dog Collar had served as a clear warning that no one was safe. Bacchus' Lair had announced it would be closed "for remodeling" for at least two weeks. And indeed a couple of the more well-off bars did go to the considerable expense of installing sprinkler systems and adding emergency exits. But for the foreseeable future, it didn't matter.

*   *   *

We had invited Bob to Chris's going away gathering, but he understandably declined, inviting us instead to dinner at his apartment on the 23rd, which we accepted with thanks. On the Saturday before Chris' departure, about twenty of our friends came over to say goodbye to Chris and to our relationship. The mood was not somber, but it was definitely subdued. There was laughter, but it was the laughter of warmth and remembrance of good times, not of wit. Several of our friends had known Ramón or others who had died with him, and there was an almost tangible sensation of an all too rare phenomenon: the recognition of the value of friendship and life, and of how brief each could be.

No one got very drunk, and there were no tears as each of the guests departed—it was as though everyone shared the unspoken agreement that tears are for the dead, not the living, and that while Chris would not be as immediately a part of their lives as he had been, he would at least still be alive.

*   *   *

We slept late on Sunday morning, after the gathering, then did the usual post-party cleaning up, washing dishes, throwing out food we'd forgotten to wrap and put in the refrigerator before we went to bed…like I said, the usual.

We treated ourselves to our last Sunday brunch, at Rasputin's. The place was busier than I'd expected, but Chris pointed out that it was daylight and many people felt relatively safer then.

I got the impression as we talked that we both felt as though we'd stepped over some sort of threshold, and that while we may no longer still have been lovers, we would indeed remain loving friends. I think we were both very grateful for that.

*   *   *

Another blurred week followed. At work I found myself increasingly fielding media requests for personal interviews. I had been instructed that any such request was to be booted up the food chain to the chief's handlers, so it wasn't my responsibility to lie through my teeth about the chief's sincere regrets that his pressing duties prevented… blah, blah, blah. With the print media, I would do my best to determine what their editors were looking for, and tailor standard press releases to the requester's specific needs and/ or questions. For the releases, I would dip into the chief's well worn little collection of acceptable, standard responses. This worked pretty well, and since those of the chief's pronouncements that were not firebombs in themselves were often ambiguous, I would choose those I thought would sound perfectly harmless on the surface, yet have potential for the strongest negative subliminal reaction from the targeted audience. I realized I was walking a tightrope, but it was worth it.

Kevin was increasingly being used as the chief's substitute for second-level requests, primarily from TV and radio talk shows. Sort of a bait-and-switch deal, but Kevin was becoming pretty effective as the chief's spokesman and he sure as hell came across as being a lot more personable. If it were Kevin running for office, even I might consider at least listening to him. I could only imagine the pressure he must be under.

On Wednesday night, while Chris was busy boxing up some of his smaller things I'd ship to him once he got settled in New York, I was surprised to answer the phone and hear Kevin's voice on the other end. I was glad it was I who took the call rather than Chris or our answering machine (which still started with "Hi, you've reached Dick and Chris…."). I didn't give a shit whether Kevin found out I was gay; it's just that his knowing would open all sorts of doorways I'd rather walk through than be pushed through.

"Kevin," I said. "This is something of a surprise."

"I know, and I'm sorry, Dick," he said, "I wouldn't be bothering you at home if it weren't important. But something has come up and I'm really not sure I know how to handle it. And having come up, I'm sure it will come up again. I really need your objective advice."

Well, that was certainly cryptic, I thought. "Of course, Kevin—that's what I'm here for. What is it?"

"I don't really feel comfortable discussing it on the phone," he said. "Could you come over to the Shelter?"

"Tonight?" I asked.

There was a pause and then: "Well, I have my prayer and meditation every evening from 10 until midnight, but if you could make it before then…" another pause, and then "…but if you would prefer to make it tomorrow morning, I'm sure it can wait until then."

With only a couple more days left for me to spend time with Chris, I really didn't feel like going out. "Well, if you really don't mind, Kevin, I am in the middle of something here, and…"

Kevin interrupted. "No, no, that's fine, Dick. Tomorrow will be fine."

"I can meet you at around nine-thirty," I said, "if that won't interfere with your schedule."

"Nine thirty will be fine," Kevin said.

But now I was really curious. "I know you don't want to go into detail on the phone, Kevin," I said, "but could you give me some idea of what it's about, so perhaps I can do some thinking about it between now and then?"

There was a long pause, and then Kevin's voice: "It's about Patrick."

*   *   *

Having called work to leave word where I'd be, I drove directly to the shelter, swinging by Marsten's to drop Chris off. He normally took the bus which ran right in front of our apartment building and dropped him off in front of the store, but by mutual unspoken agreement, we wanted to spend as much of our last days together as we could, and even a 20 minute ride into town was 20 minutes we wouldn't have had.

Though as usual there weren't many people on the streets around the shelter, once inside the doors there seemed to be a lot of activity going on. People I assumed to be volunteers were coming down the stairs with armloads of sheets, others were carrying stacks of fresh bedding back up. Tables were being scrubbed and set in the dining room, but there was no sign of Kevin. I stopped one of the passing sheet carriers to ask where I might find Reverend Rourke, and she nodded to the end of the corridor, which I assumed meant he was in his office.

As I climbed the stairs, I heard the sound of music. Piano music. I recognized it as Beethoven, but couldn't place the exact title. The door to the office was again partially open, and I saw Kevin, seated at the old upright I'd wondered about the first time I'd come into the room.

I waited until there was a pause, then knocked. Kevin swung around on the equally old piano stool and smiled, a little sadly, I thought.

"You play very well," I said as he got up to greet me. His handshake this time was…different somehow—even stronger than usual, and I got the odd impression of urgency.

"Thank you," he said, as the handshake slowed to a hand-hold. "I've always loved music." When we released hands, Kevin stepped slightly past me to close the door.

"Thanks for coming, Dick," he said. The wooden chairs, I noticed, were clear, and he gestured me to a seat. We resumed our now-accustomed positions, facing one another, but this time, rather than clasping his hands lightly between the arms of the chair, Kevin put his elbows on the arms and put his hands in the Norman Rockwell praying hands position. He lowered his head slightly until his index fingers were just inside his lips, their fingernails cradling his two front teeth. Not prayer: thought.

With his head still slightly down, he looked at me, through his long top eyelashes. He had me hooked, but I waited for him to speak first.

"I had a radio interview yesterday in Allen," he began, sitting upright, hands still in the prayer position but the index fingertips now against his lower lip, tapping it lightly.

I started to ask, *How did it go?* but it was obvious that it hadn't gone well at all.

"And...?" I said.

"And the interviewer got into some areas that both surprised and shocked me. I realized too late that he was trying to use the interview to increase his own ratings by being confrontational and obnoxious."

"And he asked you about Patrick," I said rather than asked.

Kevin lowered his hands onto the ends of the chair arms, and nodded.

"Not just questions," Kevin said. "Rude questions. Insulting questions. If I had had any idea Patrick's name would even be mentioned, I would have refused the interview from the offset. I had been told he had a reputation for hard-hitting questions, but I had no idea of how low he would stoop."

"Did your father's advisers arrange this interview?"

"No," Kevin said. "I'd gone to Allen to talk before a Citizens for Decency meeting, and at the end of the meeting, a reporter came up and asked if he could have a brief tape recorded interview. I didn't see any harm in it, so I agreed,"

"Well, that's a mistake I'm sure you'll never repeat again," I said.

Kevin sighed and said: "Obviously. My father was furious with me, and you do not want to see my father when he is furious."

He was quiet for a minute, then looked directly into my eyes. "How much do you know about Patrick?" he asked.

"That he's dead, and that he was gay," I said, honestly.

"And the rumors...?"

"About your father?" I asked. Kevin nodded. "Yes."

More silence, and then: "The fact of the matter is that now that the subject has been mentioned by one sensation-monger, there will be more. Allen isn't that big a town, but it certainly isn't that small, either. I've got six radio shows scheduled, and four TV interviews coming up in the next week." He looked at me quickly. "And, yes, all these others were arranged by my father's team."

"Well, that's something," I said, "though now that the genie's out of the bottle, there are no guarantees. How did you respond in Allen?"

"I simply said that Patrick's death had left a deep scar on our family, and that it was quite simply too painful to discuss. Most decent people would have left it at that, but he kept persisting, kept asking more and more personal questions—even mentioned that outrageous rumor."

"And your response?"

"That it was patently ridiculous, of course. I got away from him as soon as I could, but the damage had been done."

"Well, I think you did exactly what you should have done," I said. "You didn't let him get you to explode."

"Oh, but I wanted to!" Kevin said.

Again, a moment of silence, and I decided to step in. "You know, Kevin, we all should have seen this coming, and I'm rather amazed your father's people hadn't warned you. Especially in light of the Dog Collar fire. And given your father's openly hostile attitude toward gays, the fact that he had a gay son was bound to come up, and bound to be jumped on."

Kevin looked at me closely and said: "You're wondering, aren't you?"

"About what?" I asked.

"About whether I'm...a homosexual too."

"That's none of my business," I said, but wondering nonetheless. "Besides," I said, "you're married and have a child."

I meant it to be ironic, but in the back of my mind, I could hear Ramón laughing.

Kevin raised an eyebrow and cocked his head.

"Let me put the issue to rest, then," Kevin said, "by telling you something about Patrick and myself. Though we were identical twins—I'm not sure even our parents could always tell us apart—it was as though the balance of good and evil that exists in most individuals was somehow divided between us. I am not saying I'm a saint—far from it. But whereas I always knew the difference between right and wrong, between good and evil, Patrick did not. My parents did everything they could to save him from himself, but he refused their every gesture. It fell on me to be the son God had intended to give them, and that has been no easy burden, I can assure you. You cannot imagine how much trouble I got into when we were kids just because people could not tell Patrick and I apart. He would often deliberately cause trouble and then claim to be me."

I would have grinned, but thought better of it.

"But God saw me through it all," Kevin continued. "My parents suffered the torments of hell in Patrick's rebellion against—in his flaunting of—everything they had raised us to believe."

I remained silent, listening intently, as Kevin resumed his leaning forward, hands clasped over his lap pose.

"My parents are not...shall we say...demonstrative people. But I know they loved Patrick and me equally, as good Christians should. Sometimes I felt that my father loved Patrick even more, in hopes that that love would save his soul. It didn't, of course.

That Patrick drank, and lied, and cheated, and blasphemed in every possible way was bad enough. But that he was a *homosexual* as well! Can you imagine what Patrick's sexual deviancy did to a man as moral and upright as my father? And it was of course equally difficult for me; because even though he Bible clearly states that homosexuality is an abomination in the sight of God, Patrick was my brother, and I loved him. And to love him while knowing he would burn forever in the fires of hell...!"

I'd had about enough of *that* specious bullshit, so rather than tell Kevin he was full of crap, I asked:. "So what exactly happened to Patrick? Exactly how did he die?"

Kevin looked at me oddly: "That's just it," Kevin said. "He didn't,"

CHAPTER 9

I sat there for a minute before I was able to say: "Excuse me?"

"Patrick isn't dead. Not in body. But he is dead to my family and, I'm sorry to say, to me."

"I don't mean to sound dense," I said, "but what's going on here?"

Kevin gave a sad smile. "Sorry—I'm sure you are confused. I realize I'm taking a very great risk in telling you all this; you are the only person outside the family who knows. But since the story is partially out, I need to explain it all to someone who might be able to understand. I'm not sure why, but from the first time I saw you, I somehow felt you were someone I could trust. I don't have…many friends, and I really need someone I can confide in."

I almost suggested he consider his wife, but decided against it and instead said nothing

"The problem is that we have painted ourselves into something of a corner on this Patrick issue, and I need help in figuring out what to do about it."

He made it sound as though he were talking about termites in the woodwork.

"But why the charade in the first place?" I asked: "Why lie about Patrick's being dead?"

Kevin sat back in his chair. "Well, first let me ask that you promise not to tell anyone that Patrick is alive."

I nodded, and Kevin, apparently satisfied, continued. "As to why the 'charade,' as you put it, I can only say it was a domino effect. One lie—well, let's not call them lies—leads to another. As you know, my father is a man of enormous ambition—it is perhaps the greatest single force in his life. He is driven by his perceived mission to restore the fundamental moral values—which is to say, in effect, the Christian values—upon which this country was founded, He chose law enforcement as his route to this goal, and he worked himself up through the ranks."

Kevin apparently overlooked the fact that his maternal grandfather had been the city's Chief of Police for many years, and that chief Rourke's climb up the ladder could not have been hurt by this association. But again, I said nothing, and turned my attention back to Kevin.

"But." Kevin was saying, "his rise within the department was increasingly being jeopardized by Patrick's total disregard for everything he knew our father was trying to achieve. And by the time my father knew that he was in direct line for chief, Patrick's behavior was becoming totally out of control. There were two arrests—minor violations though they were—which friends of my father were able to keep from being made public. But it was clear that something had to be done.

"As you know, the police department is an extremely conservative organization…."

Gee, let me write that down, I thought. Luckily, Kevin was too deep into his story to notice the quick raising of my eyebrows.

"I know it sounds incredibly callous, but Patrick stood firmly in the way of my father's appointment. His homosexuality was becoming known outside the family and his circle of…friends.

"So my father, being an eminently practical man, made an agreement with Patrick, who had no love, respect, or sense of duty to his family. My mother had inherited a sizable fortune, and if Patrick did not love his family, he certainly loved money. So in effect, my father simply paid Patrick to disappear. An account was set up in a New York bank, from which Patrick would be able to withdraw a set amount each month on condition that he never have contact with the family again. It was made perfectly clear to him that should he be tempted to cause trouble, or to ask for more money, the annuity would cease immediately. Patrick was only too happy to agree. The 'hunting trip' scenario was devised,...."

I couldn't keep myself from interrupting: "Why? Why not just send him away, or disown him, or both? 'Killing him off' just seems too...well, melodramatic."

Kevin looked at me with mild annoyance, as though I were totally missing the point.

"You're right, of course, in retrospect. But at the time.... As long as Patrick was 'alive', attention could—and you can be sure would—be focused on him by my father's enemies," Kevin said. "They would have a continual source of live ammunition to be used against him, and I'm sure Patrick would be only too happy to supply it. But with Patrick 'dead', the issue was also dead—for anyone to try to use Patrick as a political weapon would mark them as insensitive and vindictive."

He looked at me as if for some sign that I understood. I didn't. "I'm sorry, Kevin," I said, "but I just can't help thinking that to drive a member of the family away simply because the fact of his being gay was blocking your father's career...and then to be so...again, excuse my bluntness...so hypocritical as to pretend to grieve over him...."

Kevin looked at me with a mild expression of shock. "Oh, no, Dick...no! My entire family—the younger children did not and do not to this day know any of this—truly, truly did grieve for Patrick. *I* grieved. I *still* grieve."

"And where is Patrick now?" I asked.

"I have no idea," Kevin said, but somehow I doubted that. "He has, uncharacteristically, kept his part of the agreement and has never contacted the family since that day. Money is still being withdrawn from the account each month, so we know he is alive, and I pray that he is well, and that perhaps he has found himself, if not God."

We sat for a moment in silence, and I was aware Kevin's eyes never left my face.

"It seems," I said, "as though your father has dug himself a very deep hole."

Kevin nodded. "And now we are faced with a compounded

problem. Even if we were to *try* to set the record straight at this point, it would be impossible. No one outside my family could possibly understand or, I'll readily admit, could be expected to understand. And my father's career would be destroyed."

Kevin and I simply sat and stared at one another for what seemed like an eternity. There was no *Ping! Ping! Ping!* It was a stare of searching for some sort of answer to a question that probably didn't have one.

While I loathed the chief and everything he stood for, and knew I could easily use this information to destroy him, I felt oddly sorry for Kevin and didn't relish the idea of betraying his trust. I realized, too, that the chief was pretty much his own worst enemy when it came to his actual chances for election, and assumed the voters would be smart enough to realize it and choose the senator in the primaries. And, I decided, if worse came to worst, I could use Patrick's story as a last-ditch move to keep the chief from winning.

Finally, I sat up straight to stretch my back, and since Kevin obviously wanted some sort of advice, I owed it to him to be honest. I got the impression that Kevin didn't get much honesty in his dealings with his family.

"Okay. You're right…now that the subject of Patrick has been raised in the media, it will almost surely come up again. Now, I assume the questions were only about Patrick's being gay, and the rumors that your father had something to do with his death. No indication that anyone knows he's still alive?"

Kevin shook his head.

"The very first and most obvious thing you have to do…and I'm sure your father's advisors will back me on this…is to make damn sure you never get suckered into another situation like the one in Allen. Let your father's handlers take care of who you talk to and when. I hope they're smart enough not to go overboard and start asking interviewers for a list of questions in advance—that would practically shout that you have something to hide. I don't think you have any choice but to, whenever Patrick is mentioned, say basically what you said in

Allen. Don't try to *deny* that Patrick is…was…gay, but don't volunteer anything, either. And while I know it will be a strong temptation to fall back on some old standard quotes from the Bible, I would strongly suggest that you *don't*. Don't moralize! Patrick was gay; Patrick was loved; Patrick is gone—I wouldn't even use the word "dead" if I were you. Stick to that."

Kevin nodded.

"And," I said, "you'd better go over this whole thing with your father so that you don't start telling two different stories."

Kevin nodded again.

"Now," I said just to be certain I hadn't missed anything, "*no one* else knows Patrick is alive?" Kevin shook his head. "You're sure?" I prompted.

"I'm sure."

"Well, let's hope for your…" I had started to say *your father's*, but couldn't bring myself to "…sake they don't."

*   *   *

I was summoned to C.C.'s office immediately upon my return from the shelter and was surprised to once again be offered a seat. Not good.

"Your friend Kevin blew it," C.C. began. Little niceties like "Good Morning, Hardesty" would be incomprehensible to C.C. I found his emphasis on the word "friend" to be mildly disturbing.

"I heard," I said. "That was the gist of our meeting this morning."

"I'll just bet it was," C.C. said. "If I were the chief, I'd ream that kid of his a new ass hole. But it's too late for that now. Now it's up to *me* to handle the damage control."

Yeah, C.C., I thought: *it's up to YOU!*

"That Patrick Rourke was a faggot wasn't exactly a state secret, but everybody thought it was over and done with when he had the good sense to get killed. I knew it was going to come back and bite the chief on the ass, and it has."

He glared at me as though he strongly suspected that I was responsible.

"Now, I want you to tell me *everything* you two talked about, and especially what *you* told *him*."

I went into my Sheharazade mode, and proceeded to weave a detailed tale of what was, in fact, the gist of our conversation without actually mentioning many of the details: and I sure as hell didn't mention that Patrick was alive. I told him I had advised Kevin that the best thing to do was not make an issue of it, that to try to cover it up would be more damaging than treating it as casually as possible, and to respond to future questions with the basic 'Patrick was gay, Patrick was loved, Patrick is dead'—I used the word "dead" deliberately—response.

C.C. just sat there, listening, his look of total disdain never leaving his face. When I had finished, he made a great slow-motion production of reaching into his thermidor, extracting a zucchini, unwrapping it, snipping off the end, lighting it, and then making exaggerated inhaling "pup-pup-pup" sounds as he took the first long draft.

After a long moment, he laid the cigar carefully on the edge of the ashtray, and looked at me.

"Here's exactly what you're going to do, Hardesty: you're going to downplay any references to Patrick being a faggot. You're not going to send out press releases denying it. You're not going to deny it, but you're not going to make an issue of it, either. Use the sympathy ploy: make whoever asks feel like they're stomping on the Rourke family's private grief. Keep it brief. Do you understand?"

Uh, yeah, C.C. I think I understand. Thanks for coming up with that brilliant strategy all by yourself! I guess that's why you get the big bucks.

I nodded.

C.C. took another long puff on his cigar. "The State Association of Police Chiefs' annual meeting is this coming weekend. You're coming along to keep tabs on Kevin. The kid's an idiot, but the chief really needs him."

Though I'd heard from Kevin some time ago that I'd be going along on the trip, this was the first mention C.C. had made of it to me. Not "could you come" or "would you come," but "you're coming." Class all the way.

He blew a long stream of smoke in my direction. "You'll be bunking in Kevin's hotel room—we can't afford to throw money around on extra rooms."

I was once again impressed by C.C.'s charm, by his tact and diplomacy, by his concern for his employees' feelings on whether or not they were willing to give up their weekends on a minute's notice, or if they wanted to share a hotel room. But then, why ask when you can tell?

                 *   *   *

Wednesday was to be Chris' last day at work, so his coworkers threw a party for him Tuesday night. I had a frozen pizza, called Bob to see how he was doing—which had become something of a ritual—and watched TV until Chris got home around 11, fairly well smashed.

The guest bedroom was filling up with boxes of Chris's stuff, and by mutual unspoken agreement, we kept the door to that room closed. The apartment was starting to look a little bare—pictures missing from the walls, books missing from the bookcases, empty spots where knickknacks used to be. Things that had been so common I hardly paid attention to before, but now knew I was going to miss. But we both did our best not to notice, and I think each of us was grateful for the way the other was handling the whole situation.

And then it was Thursday, and our dinner with Bob. We brought a really nice bottle of wine—not that Bob didn't have a huge rack full already—and, having mentioned it to Bob earlier, Chris had stopped at the local bakery for a sinfully rich chocolate/whipped cream cake topped with fresh banana slices.

Though we had not been really close friends before the fire, it had created a strange but strong bond between the three of us left. There was a vague awareness that all three of us were dealing with loss—Bob's of course the worst, but in a sense Chris and I were losing each other too. Bob was doing as well as could be expected, and he actually laughed a couple times during the evening. Though he spoke of Ramón several times it was in a lovingly casual way, and none of us seemed to be made uncomfortable by it. Both Chris and I knew he was still hurting terribly, but he was strong enough to make it, and we had no doubt that he would.

*   *   *

The issue of Patrick Rourke's homosexuality did, as expected, create a momentary fervor in the media, and Kevin found it necessary, in his one pre-scheduled TV interview before the police chiefs' gathering, to ward off further incursions into the subject. He handled himself quite well, and the overall result was that most people did feel the family's privacy should be respected, that the past should remain in the past.

I really wasn't quite sure why I was being dragged along to the annual meeting, other than to handle the details of assuring maximum media coverage for the chief's speech before the group and another short press conference afterwards. The prospect of being in the chief's immediate presence, for however briefly we may have to be in the same building, was not a happy one, though to be honest the fact of sharing a hotel room with Kevin for two nights was somehow oddly intriguing. Something was going on with Kevin, but I honestly had absolutely no idea what that something was, and I was determined to find out.

*   *   *

And then it was Friday; Chris' and my last day together. It's kind of hard to put into words exactly how it went. Work, of course, simply went; hectic from the minute I walked in the door to the minute I walked back out again. It started with the going home. It was rather as if someone had turned on a faucet somewhere inside me, and something was draining out, leaving me with an odd, empty feeling.

Chris had our drinks waiting when I walked in the door. I noticed immediately that the dining room table was set for two, complete with candles and a bowl of flowers. It wasn't our good china or silverware, of course—they were Chris' and were already packed and put away in the guest bedroom—but it looked really nice anyway, and in an odd way, it hurt. We each did our best to be cheerful and casual, and for the most part it worked.

Chris was getting mildly nervous about his flight, as he always did, and I sat in the kitchen with him as he made my favorite meal—pork chops (nearly burnt: the crisper the better), mashed potatoes and pan gravy, and Brussels sprouts, which I knew Chris really didn't care for. He'd even set out a little hors d'oeuvres tray with cheese and crackers and a dish of my favorite creamed herring. Now I knew exactly how he felt when I handed him those damned plastic grapes.

There were quite a few phone calls—friends with last-minute good byes and Chris' promise to send his address and phone number as soon as he had them and heartfelt promises to keep in touch.

What did we talk about? I really can't remember; the same things people who have spent five years together talk about, I guess. We kept pretending it was just another evening at home, but we knew it wasn't, and the hollow feeling was still inside me.

We headed for bed around 10, since Chris had to be at the airport by 10:30 the next day, and I had to start my drive north.

We undressed in silence, watching one another, yet the usual urge for sex wasn't there for either of us. When we climbed into bed and turned out the lights, I moved closer to Chris. "Do you suppose we should take advantage of our last night?" I asked.

Chris wrapped his arms around me and snuggled closer, as he had done so many times before over the past five years. "Let's let it be something to look forward to," he said. And we held each other warmly and in silence until we both, at last, fell asleep.

CHAPTER 10

Since I had had no desire whatsoever to fly anywhere on the same airplane with either C.C. or the chief, I had volunteered to drive my (well, Chris' of course) car and bring up the boxes of press kits, signs, posters, policy papers, and assorted P.R. paraphernalia that would be needed for the two-day meeting. By leaving directly from the airport, I'd be at the hotel in plenty of time to get things set up for the 5 p.m. cocktail party that would kick off the conference. It would also give me a couple hours to myself, which I felt I was going to need.

All the last-minute rushing around and getting ready in the morning kept both Chris and me more than busy; the trip to the airport was spent mostly in reminding one another of the various things each of us should be doing, last minute instructions from Chris on not forgetting to water the plants (a chore he had taken on out of necessity when I would never remember to do it), to be sure to open all his credit card bills so I could let him know how much he owed, making sure I had the address and phone number for the hotel the company was putting him up in—right across the river from Manhattan in New Jersey; a quick bus ride through the Lincoln tunnel—until he found a place.

There was an accident on the freeway which slowed us down to a crawl for nearly a mile, and we didn't arrive at the airport until 10:20. We decided I'd better just drop Chris off at the Boarding Passenger's zone rather than try to find a parking place and go in with him. A limo just at the curb pulled out, and I swung in to take the space. I got out of the car to walk around to help Chris extricate his two suitcases and duffel bag from the pile of meeting junk in the back seat. We set them on the curb and then just stood there awkwardly, looking at one another. At last I stepped forward and grabbed him, and we exchanged a long, hard bear hug. Then we backed away, hands still on each other's shoulders.

"Call," I said.

"I will," he said. And he picked up his bags and walked into the airport without looking back. I was glad he didn't.

*   *   *

I don't remember too much of the drive north. Traffic was relatively light, and the time passed very quickly. I don't even remember much of what I was thinking about on the way. But I was very much aware of a strange sense of loss.

I stopped for lunch at one of those fast food places that, each time I go there, I swear I will never go again. And I always do. The food would have been eminently forgettable even if I'd been in a mood to remember it. But, I reassured myself, the bad food was more than offset by the lousy service.

Arriving at the hotel, I noted the "Welcome A.S.P.C." announcement on the huge roadside marquee, and the banner over the main entrance: "Welcome, Chiefs!" Valet parking was available, but someone was just pulling out of a spot in the general parking area, and I took it. Grabbing just my one suitcase out of the back seat, I locked the car and made my way under the "Welcome, Chiefs!" banner over the main entrance and into the cavernous and mostly empty lobby. Most of the convention participants had already arrived and were attending various seminars and meetings. There was a reception desk, and I stopped to pick up my official badge and materials kit—which did not, to my relief, include tickets to either the reception or the dinner.

I found the registration desk and asked if the Reverend Rourke had registered yet. I was informed he had, and I identified myself and asked for a key. The clerk gave me just the slightest raised-eyebrow, searched his records and said: "I'm sorry, sir, your name does not seem to be in our register."

Well, we're off to a great start, I thought. I asked if they could call the room, in case Kevin might be in, and luckily he was. The clerk spoke softly and rather secretively into the phone for what seemed like ten minutes, then nodded, said "Of course, Reverend Rourke," and hung up.

I was given a registration card, which I filled out feeling rather like a hooker who's been called in for the night, and upon returning it to the clerk, a key. "1410," he said. "Enjoy your stay," and he gave me a smile that all but added "Faggot."

* * *

I knocked on 1410's door but, when there was no answer to a second knock, I used my key. I could hear the shower running as I walked in. A very nice room with two large queen-sized beds, on one of which Kevin's change of clothes lay carefully arranged. I heard the water shutting off in the shower and, as I was opening my suitcase to get at a carton of cigarettes I'd carefully placed near the top, I turned to see Kevin enter the bedroom drying his hair vigorously, stark naked. I have to admit I was more than a little impressed.

Seeing me seemed to startle him, and he hastily wrapped the towel around his middle. "Dick!" he said as though completely surprised. "I didn't hear you come in."

Not as though you didn't have some idea I might be showing up, I thought.

"I knocked," I said, "but when you didn't answer, I used my key. I gather they were not expecting me."

"I'm really sorry about the mix up," he said. "I'd assumed that Mr. Carlson had made all the arrangements."

Well, that certainly explains it, I thought.

Kevin stepped over to the bed for his clothes, and as he leaned over to pick up his shorts, his towel came loose and fell to the floor. Again, I couldn't help but notice that little Kevin was a big boy. No wonder Sue-Lynn was always smiling.

Kevin uttered an embarrassed "Sorry," and quickly bent down to pick up his towel. Then, towel held before him in one hand, shorts in the other, he looked confused as to what he should do next.

"No problem," I said, and very deliberately turned back to return to my suitcase

I managed to find room in the closet to hang up my suit, shirts, and extra pants, and by that time Kevin was dressed.

"I've got to meet my father in about half an hour," Kevin said. "Would you like to have a cup of coffee with me before I go?"

"Thanks, Kevin," I said, "but I've got a lot of stuff in the car that has to be brought in, and I have to figure out where to put it all."

"Well, let me help you, then," Kevin said.

"I'd appreciate that," I said, and meant it.

*   *   *

Except for a few items, including a stack of "Rourke for Governor: Rourke for Law" bumper stickers and a large box of campaign buttons to be left on a table just inside the door of the reception/dinner hall, most of the material was put in a storeroom off the smaller room to be used the next day for the press conference. Media coverage of the dinner—and the chief's speech to the gathering—was limited by the Association's rules. C.C. had tried to bend them, of course, but to no avail.

When Kevin left to meet with the chief—and, assumedly, with C.C., whom I'd not yet seen—I contacted the hotel's services department to make sure they'd received my earlier phoned request for coffee and rolls to be provided for the press conference, which was set for 3:30 Sunday.

I left a message for C.C. at the desk, telling him that I'd arrived, where the materials were, should he need them, and how to get someone to let him into the locked storeroom. I added that I had no idea what he wanted me to do next, but that I would await word from him.

And that pretty much did it for me for the day. I was still

perfectly well aware that my presence had not, was not, and probably would not be needed, and wondered again what I was doing here. But, I told myself, if I weren't here I'd be back walking around the apartment, thinking of Chris and feeling sorry for myself.

Back in the room, I went through the packet of material I'd received at the reception desk, and noted that the press release I'd prepared on Chief Rourke's professional background, complete with photo, was included. On glancing at the program, however, I was surprised to see that the two day meeting was to end at 3 p.m. on Sunday. I was puzzled as to why, and even whether, I would be spending Sunday night here as well.

I was lying on the bed watching the news channel on TV when Kevin came in before going to the 5 p.m. reception. He seemed, once again, to be mildly surprised to see me there.

"Aren't you coming to the reception?" he asked as he stepped into the bathroom.

"No," I said simply, not adding that I had not been invited and was just as glad not to have been.

"Well, you should come," Kevin said, as he appeared at the bathroom door with a bottle of after-shave in his hand. "We could have a drink together."

That was a surprise! I thought, and Kevin smiled. "I'm not a prude, you know. I've been known to have an occasional glass of wine—though I'm sure my father disapproves. It's my one little form of rebellion, I guess. Some of Patrick must have rubbed off on me after all. And even Jesus drank wine now and then. And if you were with me, Father couldn't say anything."

Wanna bet? I thought. *Old C.C. would be all over my ass for leading you into sin.* "Thanks anyway, Kevin," I said. "But I think I'll pass."

Kevin looked disappointed, but he just shrugged, splashing after-shave into his palm and spreading it on his chin and neck. "Okay," he said.

"I'm curious," I asked as Kevin retreated to the bathroom again to finish whatever preparations he was making. "I see the meeting is over at 3:00 tomorrow; and the press conference shouldn't last more than an hour—two, with cleanup after. There'd be plenty of time for me to get back to the city tomorrow evening."

"That's what Mr. Carlson had apparently originally intended," Kevin said, still in the bathroom. "But I told him you deserved a little free time, since you'd given up your weekend, and he agreed. And since my father will be having informal meetings with the other chiefs most of the night, and I have to be here for a Monday morning prayer breakfast for an Americans for Morality meeting, I figured you might as well spend the night with me."

What's wrong with this picture? I asked myself. I knew damned well that C.C. would much prefer me to get the hell out of here at the earliest possible moment—as, as a matter of fact, would I. But Kevin was the chief's son, and whatever Kevin wanted, Kevin was to get.

He emerged from the bathroom, looking wholesome as all hell, and put on his suit jacket. "See you later, then," he said with a smile, and left.

Who the hell is this guy, I found myself wondering. The guy who walked out the door was not the Salvation's Door Kevin I'd become used to. Even his way of speaking was a lot less formal. And he drank! The Reverend Kevin Rourke was an odd onion indeed, I decided, and I had the definite feeling that there were a lot more layers in there than I could possibly know.

I had to resist the temptation, around 6 o'clock, to call Chris' hotel in New Jersey to see if he'd arrived all right. Of course I knew full well he had, but I also knew I missed him already. I'd told him where I'd be but he knew I'd be rooming with Kevin and wouldn't call unless it were an absolute emergency.

About 6:30, I went downstairs to the main bar just off the lobby. Because the entire hotel had been taken over by the meeting, and everyone was at the reception and dinner, the bar was practically deserted. I had one drink at the bar, then moved into the equally deserted restaurant. I deliberately chose the most expensive dinner on the menu, knowing that old C.C. would have a fit, but not really giving a shit whether he did or not. I charged it to the room.

I was back in the room at 9, and decided to take a shower before Kevin got back, which I didn't expect to be much before 10:30.

As usual, once I got into the shower I lost all track of time. Showers to me are a form of meditation. I just stand there and let the water drain all the tension and the bullshit of the day away. I finally came back to reality and turned off the water, sliding the glass door wide open to grab for a towel. Kevin was standing in the bathroom doorway, watching me. And I didn't have to guess where his eyes were focused.

"Kevin!" I said; "you startled the sh…the stuffing…out of me!" And I stepped partly out of the shower to reach the towel.

Kevin held his gaze for just a fraction of a second longer, then broke it, a look of embarrassment flashing quickly over his face. "I had a slight headache, and decided to get to bed early," he said. "I…I came in to look for some aspirin. I didn't mean to…."

"Hey, don't worry about it," I said. "We're all guys here. How did it go?" I asked, making no effort to cover myself, but toweling off as if he weren't five feet away.

"Fine," he said, reaching tentatively past me to get his dopp kit on the edge of the sink. "My father's speech went well, I thought. He's got a lot of support out there." He made no effort to walk back into the other room, though I could sense he made a conscious effort to keep his eyes on my face.

Wrapping the towel around my middle, I started into the bedroom, making Kevin move swiftly backward in order to let me pass.

"Want to watch a little TV before bed?" I asked.

"I don't think so," he said. "But you go ahead if you'd like."

I noticed that he was still standing there holding his dopp kit. "Did you find your aspirin?" I asked, and once again saw the look of embarrassment as he quickly set the kit on the dresser and opened it. He rummaged around for a moment, then came up with a bottle of aspirin, making a point of holding it up so that I could see it.

While he returned to the bathroom for some water, I quickly put on a pair of shorts and pulled the covers back on my bed. I was about halfway into bed when he emerged. Without a word he went to one of his suitcases and removed a neatly folded pair of pajamas. He then went back into the bathroom and closed the door.

The shower had done it for me, and I was close to nodding off when Kevin came out of the bathroom in his pajamas and hung up his clothes. I remembered his telling me once that he always meditated and prayed between 10 and midnight; I wondered if he did it in his pajamas.

He got into bed. "No TV?" he asked.

"Nah, I don't think so," I said. "I'm about out."

"Okay," Kevin said as he reached over to turn out the light between the beds. "Good night, Dick."

"Good night, Kevin."

I was just about asleep when I heard a soft sound...a sort of "Mmmmm." I swam back to consciousness and tuned my ears to the sound. though I did not move my head, which was facing away from the other bed. A moment later it came again: "Mmmmmm.....mmmmmmmm ... ahh."

I was sure as hell wide awake *now*. The "Mmmmm"'s became just a little louder and faster, and it sure didn't sound like prayer and meditation to me. And I was aware of definite movement in the next bed. Then the "Mmmmm"'s were mixed with short gasps of breath, coming faster and faster and then a sharp "Uh! Uh! Uhhhhh!!" And then silence.

Kevin was jacking off, and the bastard knew damned well I knew it!

CHAPTER 11

I awoke to the sound of the shower and glanced at my watch on the night-stand. It was 6:45. I just lay there for a while, thinking about last night. I wasn't sure yet just what game Kevin thought he was playing, but I wanted to be sure he knew I was aware of it.

A few minutes after I heard the shower turn off, Kevin entered the room, towel wrapped around his waist. Noticing I was awake, he gave me a smile and a cheerful:"Good morning, Dick."

"'Morning, Kevin," I replied. "Sleep well?"

"I only wish Sean slept as well," he said. "You?"

"Great," I said, then added: "Have any trouble getting to sleep?"

Not a flicker of embarrassment or any reaction whatever from Kevin as he removed shorts and socks from his suitcase and prepared to return to the bathroom. "None at all," he said nonchalantly. "I dropped right off as soon as my head hit the pillow."

Uh-huh, I thought.

*   *   *

About 5 minutes after Kevin left to meet his father for breakfast and church, the room phone rang. It was C.C. at his usual bubbling-good-mood best.

"Hardesty!"

"Good morning, Mr. Carlson," I said in my best lackey voice.

"You spent all yesterday sitting on your duff, and today it's time you earned your keep. I want you in that meeting room from one o'clock on. You see anybody with a reporter's badge, or carrying TV equipment, you bust your ass to find out if they need anything and if they do, make sure they get it. Is that clear?"

"Of course." I knew damned well he expected me to add a "Mr. Carlson" or "Sir" but I just wasn't going to play along.

"The conference is at 3:30. I want the coffee there by 2:45. Did you arrange for the coffee?"

"Last week," I said. "And rolls, as you told me at the time. And I checked with Guest Services when I got in yesterday. Everything is ready."

"Well, you'd just better be damned sure it is," he said, and hung up.

*   *   *

The press conference went without a hitch. The coffee was there, the rolls were there, the reporters were there— though considerably fewer than C.C. had apparently anticipated from the number of contacts we'd made and the amount of P.R. material I'd brought along. The chief's speech had obviously been scripted and rehearsed and polished until it glittered, and I tried very hard not to hear a single word of it. Whenever I did catch a sentence or two, it was the usual call for a new era in government with greatly expanded law enforcement powers to protect the citizenry from those who flaunt with impunity etc. ad nauseam.

He even made it through the question period relatively unscathed. There were far fewer questions about the fire—partly because this was a statewide representation of the media, with I believe two reporters from the networks and a couple stringers for papers outside the state. A few of the questions alluded to the chief's right-wing attitudes, but he was obviously prepared for them and managed to sidestep around them or obscure them in ambiguity.

And that was it. The reporters left, the chief left, C.C. left (without even a nod of acknowledgment that I was in the room),

Kevin and the chief's handlers and cronies left, and I was, again, left to clean up the mess.

As I was carrying a box of unused publicity materials back to the car, Kevin stopped me in the lobby.

"I think that went very well," he said with a smile. "Thanks for your help getting everything set up."

"Thanks." Now there's a word I don't think I'd ever heard before in the term of my employment with Carlton Carlson & Associates.

"I've got to run," Kevin said, "but wondered if you might do me a favor?"

"Sure," I said. "What?"

"Well, I've got to join my father and Mr. Carlson and some of the chiefs for dinner, but I thought that when I got back to the room, it might be nice to relax for a while and celebrate with a small bottle of wine. Would you mind picking one up? And I hope you'll consider sharing it with me."

"What kind would you like?" I asked, hoping my bafflement wasn't too obvious.

"I really don't know; I seldom drink. But perhaps a Sauvignon?"

"Sure," I said.

And with a smile and a small wave, he moved off in one direction while I continued in the other, wondering for the hundredth time what in hell was going on.

Look, I'm not exactly new to this game. I've done my share of cruising, and I've been cruised from time to time, and I've always felt pretty confident as to who was doing what with whom. But with Kevin.... *Was* he coming on to me? Or was I just imagining it because Kevin—if you set aside just about everything he stood for—was kind of hot in his own way, and with Chris being gone, I might be looking for a little rebounding?

I reached the car, opened the trunk, and put the box inside. But what straight guy jacks off with another guy in the next bed? Was it supposed to have been some sort of invitation? I'd never given Kevin any overt hints about my being gay, and no one has ever pointed a finger at me and said *"There's* one!" Of course it's one of the oldest clichés in the book that we can always spot one another a mile off. And Patrick was gay, and Patrick and Kevin are identical twins. And….

I returned to the hotel for the rest of the materials to be taken back to the office, and managed to fit everything in the trunk. Then, as long as I was out, I drove around looking for a liquor store. Share a bottle of wine, eh? Well, whatever his game was, he had me hooked—let's see where he was going from here.

* * *

I started out to have dinner in the hotel dining room again, but as I came up to the door, I noticed that not only were there a lot more diners in the room, but that one large table included C.C., the chief, Kevin, and several others. I decided to take the car and go down the street to a seafood restaurant I'd seen while looking for the liquor store earlier.

Good drinks, good food, and a really hot waiter who cruised me pretty blatantly. I noticed he was wearing a wedding ring. I guess you just never can tell….

Making sure I got a receipt, I left the restaurant and returned to the hotel at around 9:45. Kevin was seated in one of the small armchairs, watching TV. He gave me a very brief but undisguised *"Where have you been?"* look, but then quickly smiled and said: "I didn't see you in the dining room."

"I decided to get out for some air," I said. "I put the wine on the wet bar. Did you find it?"

"Yes, but I thought I'd wait for you before I opened it."

"Are you ready for it now?" I asked, hoping to hell it didn't sound quite like the double entendre I heard the minute it left my mouth.

Kevin rose from the chair and went into the bathroom. "We'll have to use the glasses in here," he said.

"No problem for me," I said, and walked over to the wet bar for the wine. I know it's really gauche, but I like wine—any wine—chilled. But not knowing Kevin's preferences, I had not put it into the small refrigerator under the wet bar. But I did check to see if there were ice cubes, and was surprised to see that there were. Fancy place.

As I picked up the wine, I suddenly realized we didn't have a corkscrew. Kevin, returning to the room with the unwrapped glasses, saw my look of confusion, and deduced the problem.

"The Boy Scouts to the rescue," he said, setting down the glasses on the small table near the window and moving to his dopp kit, from which he extracted a large Swiss Army type knife. "These thing *do* come in handy," he said, producing a corkscrew from the assortment of slots.

The television set had a "music only" option, which Kevin selected, adjusting the volume to listenable but not intrusive. We sat at the table and Kevin poured the wine, then held up his glass. "Cheers," he said.

I raised my glass and clicked it lightly against his. "L'Chaim."

We actually had a nice conversation, and he was considerate enough not to let his religious enthusiasms run wild. He talked of his childhood with Patrick, and of how close they had been until puberty, when Patrick's behavior began its downward slide. While he didn't come directly out and say so, it wasn't hard to deduce that he and Patrick had provided for one another the affection they did not get from their parents. Oddly, I got the distinct impression that Kevin was almost envious of Patrick's rebellion against their parents, and resentful of the attention that that rebellion brought Patrick.

He talked of meeting Sue-Lynn, the daughter of Mrs. Rourke's college roommate and how strongly, with Patrick not only gone but gay, he felt the obligation to provide his parents with the grandchild they expected of him. "Sue-Lynn and I have a very special, loving Christian relationship," he said—but I did not get the impression that true love had that much to do with it. And of course he worshipped Sean. His work with the Salvation's Door took up the vast bulk of his time, and he again said without saying that being away from it as frequently as was now necessary was not something he enjoyed.

But above all, I was impressed by the fact that Kevin never once mentioned having a real friend of his own. I sensed an intense loneliness in him, and that in turn made me feel strangely sad.

It was after eleven—obviously his prayer and meditation routine was not written in stone—when we finished the wine, and I could tell Kevin was feeling it. We decided to call it a night, since Kevin had to get up early, and I wanted to be back in the city by noon.

So while Kevin went into the bathroom, I stripped down to my shorts and climbed into bed. I was surprised to see Kevin come back into the room wearing just his shorts. "I spilled something on my pajamas," he explained. I noticed, as he got into bed, how nicely he filled out the front of his shorts.

"Good night, Dick," he said.

"Good night, Kevin," I replied, and he reached over to turn out the light.

Again, just as I was about to drift off, I heard sounds from the other bed. A second later, I felt the sheets on my own bed being lifted and realized Kevin was climbing into bed with me. I turned over onto my back and started to sit up.

"Kev…" I started to say, but he was lying beside me, now, one hand on my chest.

"Shhhhhhh," he said, and his hand moved down my chest, across my stomach, and under the waistband of my shorts.

I just lay back in total surprise, and felt his mouth and tongue follow the path his hand had set. Instinctively I raised my hips so he could slide my shorts down.

"Kevin, are you sure…" I whispered.

"Oh, God, yes," Kevin whispered in return, and we both moaned loudly as his mouth consumed me. He proceeded to bring me to one of the most shudderingly violent climaxes I can ever remember having.

As I regained my breath, he moved back up and kissed me gently on the lips. I reached down, fumbling for him, but he pushed my hand away.

"No," he said, and slipped quickly out of my bed and back into his own.

The silence was broken only by the sound of our breathing, and after a long, long time, I drifted off to sleep.

*   *   *

I awoke once again to the sound of the shower and took a quick, automatic-reflex look at my watch—it was again 6:45. I lay in something of a stupor, thinking about the previous night. What in *hell* had *that* been all about? I wondered. Not that I was unhappy with what had happened. Far from it—Kevin had a definite talent outside his day job. But...

The sound of the shower shutting off cut my thoughts short, and I just lay there, thinking nothing at all. Finally Kevin emerged from the bathroom.

"Good morning, Dick," he said brightly, flashing me a big smile.

"Good morning, Kev," I said.

Kevin smiled. "Patrick used to call me that when we were kids," he said. "That's the first time anyone's called me 'Kev' in a long, long time." He was silent only a moment, then said "How did you sleep?"

"Never better," I lied. And then something prompted me to ask: "And you?"

"Like a baby," he said. "I guess that wine really relaxed me. I hardly remember lying down."

Oh-oh, I thought, *not the old 'I was so drunk I don't remember a thing' routine.* But suddenly I had the almost frightening feeling that Kevin wasn't lying. And it didn't have anything to do with being drunk.

CHAPTER 12

All the way back to the city I tried to keep my mind *off* Kevin
Rourke, Chief Rourke, Patrick Rourke, and the entire Rourke
clan. They were, without a doubt, a truly fucked up family. In
a strange way—particularly after last night—I felt strong
empathy for Kevin. I suspect if a good psychiatrist ever got his
hands on Kevin, he'd have material for about ten books. The
pressures on him were almost incomprehensible to me. The
question of whether Kevin was or was not gay himself was, as
far as I was concerned, pretty well resolved by last night's little
episode—but the thing that kept niggling at me was whether
Kevin knew he was gay. With a father like Chief Rourke, no
wonder Patrick and Kevin went two totally opposite paths. Kevin
desperate to please, to live up to what he thought was expected
of him; Patrick having that extra ounce of whatever it takes to
say: "Fuck this!" and to do something about it.

Well, that was their problem, and the sooner I got a life of
my own back, the better I'd like it.

*   *   *

I went directly to the office, where I was told C.C. had called
in to announce he would not be coming in at all that day. Of
course, he didn't give an explanation. Explanations are for the
little people.

I had received that morning a phone message from Charles
McNearny, who was Joseph Goebbels to the chief's Adolph
Hitler, and was one of the major puppeteers of the chief's bid
for governor. McNearny, I'd learned through the office
grapevine, was a close golfing buddy of C.C., and was probably
far more heavily instrumental in C.C.'s getting the P.R.

assignment than C.C. would ever admit. I decided to give him a call immediately, so I could let C.C. know that I hadn't wasted another whole day of his time.

McNearny was executive director of the state's Grading Contractors and Engineers Association—an incredibly powerful lobby in the state capitol. Funds for road construction had, under the current governor, been significantly cut back, the governor preferring to fritter away the state's money on frivolous things like schools.

I reached McNearny's secretary who, after I identified myself, rather surprisingly put me directly through to the man himself.

"Mr. Hardesty!" the voice was warm, sincere, confident—the kind of voice that makes me want to check to see if my wallet's still there. "I'm really glad you called."

I explained that I'd just returned from the S.A.P.C. meeting, which of course he knew without my telling him.

"Wonderful. We all appreciate the work you and Carlton are doing on the chief's campaign."

"That's kind of you to say," I said; but my mind was telling me that this was a man to watch out for.

"Young Kevin tells me that you have an idea for a fund raiser for Salvation's Door that might help boost the chief's image in the public's eye."

"Yes, sir," I said. This was also a man I did not want to alienate, I knew. "It seems like a good way to show Chief Rourke's involvement in community projects."

"Well, it is an interesting idea. Tell you what, why don't you and I and Kevin get together—for dinner, let's say—and talk about it?"

"That would be fine, Mr. McNearny, if you can find the time."

"When it comes to putting Chief Rourke into the governor's seat, Dick…you don't mind if I call you Dick, do you…" He did not wait for a reply. "…I can always find the time. How about tomorrow evening, say around 7:00 at the Imperator?"

"That will be fine, sir," I said. "I look forward to meeting you in person."

"And I you, Dick...and I you. See you there, then," and he hung up. *Step into my parlor, said the spider to the fly.*

The Imperator was definitely *not* my kind of place. It was one of those restaurants where the guests are given menus without prices and of course I had never been inside the doors—nor had anyone else that I knew. Still, it was intriguing, and obviously an effort to impress or intimidate, depending upon the host's intentions. And I pretty much knew what this host's intentions were.

But I still couldn't figure out why. Why I should be dragged along to a big meeting of police chiefs when I did practically nothing; why Kevin should be so strongly on my side (well, the reason for that one wasn't all that hard to figure out, I guess); and why C.C. should have appointed me to be, in effect, Kevin's little friend?

I told the secretary that I would be working at home for the rest of the day, and left.

*   *   *

It was a strange feeling, walking into the apartment for the first time, knowing that Chris was gone. An odd, empty feeling. But I realized this was the way it was going to be and I'd just better get used to it. I set my suitcase inside the door, and went directly to the answering machine. Quite a few calls, two of them from Chris.

He'd arrived on time Saturday, and was calling from the airport, just to let me know he had indeed arrived safely, even though he knew I wouldn't be home. The second call was Sunday night, when he thought I just might be home. He'd spent the day going through the "Apartments for Rent" ads, and was totally depressed. He'd known that going from paying half the rent here to paying all the rent in New York would take a huge bite out of his raise, but hadn't realized just how huge a chunk that was likely to be, and was afraid he'd actually end up with less money than he'd been making here.

I started to pick up the phone to call him, but realized he'd undoubtedly be out meeting with people from the store, or apartment hunting. So I decided I'd give him a call later on to offer moral support...besides, I wanted to hear his voice.

There was a call from Bob asking me to join him for dinner that night, and I called him right back to accept. I didn't feel like spending much time in the apartment just then. We agreed to eat out, since neither of us had even begun to adjust to batching it.

                              *   *   *

I called Chris just before leaving the apartment to meet Bob, and caught him just as he was ready to leave the hotel to see "The Fantastics," his first time in a New York theater—off Broadway, of course, but the excitement was still there. He had spent the day apartment hunting to no avail but was determined to keep at it. So we just had time to exchange quick encapsulated bits of news and hung up, promising to talk later in the week.

My dinner with Bob was rather nice, actually, and I think it did us both a lot of good. Up until the night of the Dog Collar fire, we'd never spent any time together except as a foursome. And while he and I would usually spend a lot of time talking with one another while Chris and Ramón did the same, it was still different to be just the two of us. I got the distinct impression that we were going to become pretty good friends.

Bob's big news of the evening was that he had heard at long last from his insurance company, and it seemed they were fairly close to getting off the fence—though he still wasn't sure which side they'd come down on. I told Bob of my weekend—leaving out the part about Kevin's crawling into bed with me—and of my growing Reptile House fascination with the whole Rourke family. I also, of course, didn't mention that Patrick was alive.

                              *   *   *

C.C. had, apparently, had selective short-term amnesia. When he came blustering through the office on Tuesday morning, he nearly knocked me over as I was heading back from the copy machine with a stack of press releases. I certainly didn't expect an "excuse me," but thought he perhaps might have recognized me as the guy who'd just given up his weekend for the team. Silly me.

But about ten seconds after I'd returned to my desk, my phone rang. "I want to see you in my office."

I did my little knocking twice routine, and got the usual curt: "Come."

I took my usual stance—emphasis on stance—just inside the door, about halfway between it and C.C.'s enormous glistening walnut desk, which was about the size of a pool table. It's polished top contained one telephone, one Rolodex, one mahogany thermidor, one photo of Mrs. C.C. and Junior C.C., for whom I had the utmost sympathy, one pen holder, with pen, and one sheet of paper, to give the impression C.C. was busily at work. I rather suspected it was always the same sheet of paper, but never got close enough to check.

"You're having dinner with Charles McNearny tonight," he said.

Yes, I know, I thought. But I'd learned that C.C. had an aversion to question marks. I think he thought it would make him appear vulnerable.

"The Imperator," he said. "You're swimming with some pretty big fishes now, Hardesty, and you'd damned well not do anything to embarrass this firm."

Does that mean I can't wear the bib overalls? I thought, but said nothing.

"The important thing for you to understand here is that what Charles McNearny says in regards to what will or will not be done to promote the chief is the way it will be. If you disagree with anything he says, you just keep your mouth shut and nod your head 'yes.' You got that?"

"Got it," I said.

He gave me that palm-down flick of his fingers which so subtly indicated that our lesson for the day was over. I turned and walked out the door without looking back.

*   *   *

I arrived at the Imperator at exactly 7:00. Of course, I'd gotten to the place fifteen minutes earlier, parked in a public garage, and just sat there for awhile in order to time my entrance to the minute. I must admit that I was impressed: the place reeked of elegance but without overpowering you with it. Lots of heavy, rich carved wood, soft lighting, walls hung with pictures you knew automatically were not prints; thick, burgundy carpets with a quiet blue pattern of some sort. I stepped to the maitre d's podium, announced myself and asked if Mr. McNearny or Reverend Rourke had arrived. I was again very impressed by the fact that the maitre d', though he looked the stereotype, was actually friendly and smiled readily.

Since 7 p.m. was practically the break of day for most of the Imperator's patrons, the dining room was relatively empty, and as soon as the maitre d' led me down the short staircase into the main room, I spotted Kevin seated with a man I'd seen only in photographs. Both men stood up as I approached the table. Kevin and I shook hands first, and then I was introduced to Charles McNearny.

"Dick Hardesty," McNearny said, voice deep with warmth and good fellowship; "a pleasure to meet you!"

'Thank you, Mr. McNearny; it's a pleasure meeting you, too."

As we sat, McNearny gave a nod to no one in particular and a waiter appeared as if out of the genie's lamp, a bottle of wine wrapped like a baby in white linen cradled in one arm.

"I hope you don't mind," McNearny said nodding again to set the waiter into his uncorking/decanting ritual, "but I've always enjoyed this particular vintage and took the liberty of ordering it for us."

While all this was going on, I took stock of Charles Mc-

Nearny. Deeply tanned, impeccably groomed and dressed; quite handsome by corporate boardroom standards. I recognized immediately that he gave new meaning to the word "Confidence man"—he practically oozed it, and it was undoubtedly the reason he headed up one of the state's most powerful lobbying organizations.

"So tell me, Dick," McNearny began, "are you married?"

"Separated," I said truthfully. I caught Kevin's quick sidelong glance, but it was so swift I hoped McNearny hadn't noticed.

*   *   *

The dinner conversation was casual, wide ranging at first and finally funneling down to the chief's campaign. The bulk of the conversation was between Kevin and McNearny, of course, since they'd known each other for some time. My own contributions were mainly generalizations.

The food was, of course, superb; the service that perfect balance of anticipation of needs without being intrusive.

When the desert cart was brought over, filled with such wonders as to make the arteries harden just by looking at them, I was too full to take advantage of it, and opted just for coffee, as did Kevin and, after encouraging us to change our minds about desert, McNearny.

Finally, over coffee, McNearny apparently decided it was time to get to the point. "Kevin tells me you don't think too much of Chief Rourke's public image."

Pushing aside a mental image of C.C. toppling over in apoplexy, I plunged right in.

"It's not what I think that matters," I said; "it is what the rest of the voting public thinks and, frankly, since the chief is so…private a person…the average man on the street only knows what he reads in the newspapers and sees on TV. And to him, the chief is little more than an imposingly authoritarian figure in a police chief's uniform—with all negative images those things bring to mind."

McNearny smiled. "You're absolutely right," he said. "Kevin told me you weren't afraid to tell it like it is."

I wasn't quite sure whether I could breathe a sigh of relief or not, so I held off.

"I've known Chief Rourke for a good long time now, and I sincerely believe he is exactly the man this state desperately needs in the governor's mansion. But I have no illusions about how he comes across to the average voter. The Sunday Supplement article you and Carlton did was exactly the kind of thing we need to…well, to show there's a human being under that uniform. The timing could not have been worse with the bar fire incident, but that could not have been foreseen, and we have to move on." He took a drink of his coffee, then carefully set it back on its saucer before looking back at me. "Exactly how do you picture this fund-raiser scenario?"

Once again I had the mildly disturbing feeling that I might actually be helping the chief, but ego does strange things, so I forged ahead.

"Obviously, it would have to be a fund-raiser for Salvation's Door, not for the chief's campaign coffers." I didn't know whether McNearny knew the chief owned the building, and that obviously any improvements that might result would ultimately benefit him and thereby provide a solid basis for conflict of interest charges. I knew full well that if he did know, McNearny was shrewd enough to recognize that little time bomb and would jump right in, but he said nothing. I also thought Kevin might take the opportunity to mention it, but he didn't. Whether the chief himself would see the danger here was another matter altogether, but I suspected he might just be arrogant and self-serving enough to think no one would find out.

"The actual event could be as low-key or as big a deal as you and the chief's other advisers might choose to make it," I continued. "But I might suggest a low-key approach; holding the event at the shelter itself rather than at some ballroom. Let those attending see just how the homeless actually live—I'm sure most of them have no idea. Maybe even instead of a caterer, serve the same lunch the homeless receive —which I can attest, is pretty good given what Kevin has to work with. The important thing is that the public see the chief in surroundings not directly linked to his job. It would also shore up his image as a family man showing his support for his son, and it certainly would help Kevin continue his work for the homeless."

McNearny sat there nodding as I talked, and I noted that Kevin was looking at him intently, as if watching for his reaction.

"Interesting," McNearny said at last, and I saw Kevin almost imperceptibly relax. "Of course there are certain problems we'd have to overcome. One of the chief's greatest problems, I think we all realize, is that while he is a decisive leader, his intense devotion to his duty and sense of purpose makes him appear...well... uncomfortable in actual face-to-face meetings with people he does not know well. We realized going in that this would be an obstacle, and I even went so far as to recommend he hire someone to help him to be more at ease in group situations in which he is not giving orders. But I think we just might be able to do something with this. Let me talk it over with a few of the others, and we'll let you know."

The meeting/dinner/whatever it was supposed to be broke up shortly thereafter. Kevin had to return to the shelter to take care of some unfinished business from the day, and McNearny said he had an early flight to the capitol the next day to lobby a group of senators for a proposed highway in the state's relatively undeveloped north.

We left the restaurant together and went our separate ways. I got the feeling Kevin wanted to talk with me privately, but he said nothing as we shook hands and said our good-nights.

*   *   *

I was more wound up from the meeting than I'd thought and decided that rather than return directly home, I'd stop in at Griff's, a piano bar on the way, for a quick one to help me sleep when I did get home. It was only a little after 9:30 when

I arrived at the bar, found a parking place easily on the nearly deserted street, and went in. As I expected, the place was very sparsely populated; maybe five guys at the bar and three around the piano, where one of my favorites, Guy Prentice, was holding sway. I ordered my drink and noticed a familiar large, dark form at one of the stools surrounding the piano.

I walked over to the piano, smiled and nodded to Guy, who returned both, and sat at the stool next to Tondelaya/ Teddy, who was engrossed in conversation with an anorexic-looking bleached blond on the other side of him.

As I said, Guy was one of my—and Chris'—personal favorite bar performers. Guy knew every song—melody and words—from every musical produced on Broadway from 1922 to the present. He loved the campier numbers and spending an evening listening to him was always a delight.

The blond on the other side of T/T drained his glass, pushed himself off the barstool, and he and T/T exchanged over-the-top "Mmmmm-*wah* mmmmm-*wah*" cheek kisses. With regal waves to Guy, the bartender, and the room in general, he made his way to the door and disappeared. T/T settled back on his stool and for the first time noticed my presence. He gave a melodramatic jerk backward, eyes wide open. "Why chile, where did you come from?"

"The stork brought me, I'm told," I said.

T/T slapped at my arm and grinned, then looked around. "Where's your other half?"

"He's in New York," I said.

"Oh, that lucky boy!" T/T said. "When's he comin' back?"

I tried to be as casual as possible when I said "He's not. He got a great promotion and we decided he should take it."

T/T laid his hand gently on my arm, his eyes wide in a look of surprise. "You mean you two…?"

I nodded.

"Well, darlin', I'm sorry. I truly am. But look on the bright side: somewhere out there's two very lucky guys who're goin' to find the both of you."

That was really nice of him to say, I thought. "Thanks, Teddy," I said. Noticing his glass was nearly empty, I said "Can I buy you a drink?"

His face broke into a broad grin. "Why of *course* you can, darlin'."

I caught the bartender's attention and pointed to T/T's glass. He nodded and turned to make the drink.

"Something you'd like to hear, Dick?" Guy asked.

"Yeah," T/T said. "You play this boy 'Maybe This Time.'"

Guy raised his eyebrows in an unspoken question, and I gave him a small grin and a nod. It certainly wasn't the song I'd have chosen under the circumstances, but T/T meant well, and I appreciated the gesture. T/T and Guy sang it together, with T/T's large arm draped around my shoulder.

Guy then segued into a "Cabaret" medley as the bartender came over with T/T's drink. "Thank you, darlin'," T/T said, raising his glass in a toast. I raised mine and tapped it against his, and we sat quietly for a few minutes listening to Guy play.

"So when, exactly, is Bacchus' Lair going to reopen?" I asked.

"A week this coming Friday, I hear," T/T said. "Can't be too early for me...I don't like bein' out of work."

"I can imagine," I replied. Another moment of silence, and I let my curiosity get the better of me for the ten thousandth time.

"Who actually owns Bacchus' Lair?" I asked.

T/T shrugged. "I honestly don't know, darlin'. Whoever it is, I've never met him. Dave Lee runs the place. He's a good manager, but he sort of keeps his distance."

"Like Judy," I observed.

T/T gave me a strange look, and said nothing.

"What *do* you know about Judy?" I asked.

T/T took a quick drink and set his glass carefully down on the napkin in front of him. He didn't look directly at me as he said: "I don't know nothin' about Judy, darlin'. Nothin' at all, and I prefer to leave it that way."

CHAPTER 13

Wednesday morning I got to my desk to find a phone message from Kevin, ostensibly requesting that I stop by the shelter with some P.R. materials for him to take on his next speaking-for-the-chief jaunt. I suspected he really wanted to talk about dinner with McNearny, or perhaps to offer some sort of explanation for his little bed-hopping adventure at the S.A.P.C. meeting.

One of the nice things about working within the outer fringes of the Rourke camp was that I had a lot more flexibility than most of C.C.'s other workers-in-the-vineyard. I did a couple minor jobs around the office, then told the secretary I had to run over to Kevin's with the materials he requested. I timed it to arrive at the shelter around 10:15, knowing that Kevin would not have much time to talk before the 11:00 lunch hour.

Seated in Kevin's office he got right to the point: "I think last night went very well," he said, "and Charles seemed quite impressed by your presentation. But something has been bothering me a bit…"

This was the first time Kevin and I had been alone since the meeting, and I was again wondering if he might be going to allude to just what he thought was going on between the two of us.

"What's that?" I asked.

"Well, I believe I told you my father owns this building, and it occurred to me that some people might see a fund-raiser for the shelter as something of a conflict of interest. To raise money for improvements of a building he actually owns…"

Wrong again, Hardesty, I thought. "You gave me the impression that very few people knew your father owned the building," I said. "Is it in his name?" I asked.

Kevin shook his head. "No, it's under GenisisCorp, a

corporation my parents established many years ago for tax purposes when they began investing in real estate."

"And does McNearny know about GenisisCorp or that it owns this building?"

"I don't think so. Like most things, my parents prefer to keep their business dealings private. But…"

"Well, then, I think to cover the eventuality of someone finding out and raising a fuss, we should make a point of stressing that the fund-raiser is strictly for operating expenses, food, etc.; things that would not in themselves enhance the building's value. That way, if anyone did find out, it wouldn't matter."

"Do you think I should bring this up with Charles?" Kevin asked.

I thought a minute before answering. "Maybe you should let that be up to your father. If McNearny and his team don't already know, it's your father's choice to tell them or not."

At this point there was a knock at the office door, and the same skeletal form who had interrupted one of our earlier meetings stood again in the doorway.

"Yes, John?" Kevin asked.

"It's the oven again, Reverend. Sorry to bother you, but…"

"No problem, John. Make sure everything's shut off, and I'll be down in just a moment."

John nodded, turned, and disappeared, wiping his hands on his apron. Kevin looked at me, shrugged, and got up from his chair. I followed suit

"Thanks again, Dick," Kevin said. "You don't know how much it means to have somebody I can talk openly to."

Once again I found myself really feeling kind of sorry for the guy. "Any time, Kev," I said. We shook hands and I followed him down the stairs, noting a very faint odor of gas coming from the kitchen.

*   *   *

There was a message from Chris on my machine when I got home announcing that he had finally found a furnished single apartment he liked and could afford—barely, and that he was moving in the next day and would call me again as soon as he got his phone put in. He added that he loved his new job, and I was happy that he was obviously making the transition smoothly.

Tom had also called and left a message, asking if we could meet for dinner Thursday night. I called him back immediately, only to get *his* machine. I assumed from the tone of his voice that he had some news about the Dog Collar investigation, and was anxious to talk with him. I suggested we meet around seven at O'Grunion's Grill, a popular mostly straight but gay friendly restaurant about halfway between his house and mine, and for him to call me with an alternate place if O'Grunion's wasn't convenient.

I made myself a drink, fried up a hamburger patty I'd taken out of the freezer that morning, and fixed a box of macaroni and cheese. It wasn't the Imperator, but it was home.

* * *

Dinner with Tom revealed that while the Dog Collar fire was almost certainly the work of the same arsonist as the other six fires, there were some puzzling differences. The bottle used to hold the gas was not a Valley Vineyards Chianti bottle, but from what they could determine from the glass fragments and lid they'd managed to find, a large, gallon-sized jar used mostly by bars and restaurants for condiments such as mayonnaise or jumbo olives—they were trying to determine which. The jar lid had had a quarter-sized hole drilled or punched in it to fit the cloth wick. The arsonist had apparently wanted to make sure that it created the largest possible bang, and it had done just that.

What was most puzzling and disturbing to the arson investigators was of course the fact that in the previous six bombings the arsonist had taken great care to assure that no one would be hurt. The fires had been carefully timed for after closing when no one was around. With the Dog Collar, there was not the slightest doubt that the bomb was meant to kill, and to kill as many as possible.

Tom suspected that the arsonist was familiar with the Dog Collar's layout, which opened up the unthinkable but unavoidable possibility that the arsonist might be someone from the community. The police, of course, liked this idea a lot—it could shift their focus from hate groups to the chief's "jealous boyfriend" scenario and give them a good reason to hassle the fire's survivors.

The Dog Collar's office was located directly to one side of the rear exit, and had a window facing the alley. Though barred, it could have been used to pour gas onto the inside wall as windows had in previous fires. Instead, the arsonist had risked being seen by opening the back door—which was, Tom noted, a fire door with an interior bar release which could not be opened from the outside. Tom speculated that the arsonist had to have been waiting in the alley for someone to come out, and then managed to slip some sort of a wedge to keep it from closing all the way.

The stairway leading down to the dungeon was just inside the rear door and was the only way in or out of the basement. Using the door rather than the office window guaranteed that anyone in the dungeon would be trapped there, as they were. The fifteen bodies burned beyond recognition were all found in the dungeon.

The six previous fires had merely been arson. The Dog Collar was, clearly, calculated mass murder.

*   *   *

Friday morning C.C. summoned me to his office.

"There will be a fund-raiser to raise money for the Salvation's Door homeless shelter a week from Sunday," C.C. announced.

No shit, Dick Tracy! I thought.

"Ostensibly," C.C. continued in his best Sermon on the Mount voice, "it will be to raise money for the shelter, but its primary purpose is to show the chief as a caring, concerned citizen supporting his son. We'll play up the 'man of the people' angle to the hilt—hold the fund-raiser right in the shelter, show the chief eating the same food the they serve the bums. I just hope he doesn't gag on it. Charles McNearny and I will be working together on the details, but it's up to me to whip the whole thing into shape."

Uh-huh.

"Sunday afternoon's a piss-poor time to have a fund-raiser from the point of maximizing press coverage, but it's the only time of day the place won't be crawling with bums and winos. As it is, it'll have to be crammed in between their regular meals and it'll take some pretty fancy footwork.'

Let me guess whose feet, I thought.

"Now, the chief's kid thinks the fund-raiser should be only for food and supplies, but from what I hear the place is a total dump and needs a complete renovation. The chief should thank his lucky stars I'm in charge of public relations and not his kid—he can't see beyond the end of his nose: no concept of the big picture. So here's what you're going to do: you're going to have your buddy Kevin call R&D Contractors…are you listening to me, Hardesty?" he demanded.

Oh, I was listening, all right. "R&D Contractors," I repeated.

"Right." He reached into his thermidor for a zucchini. Ignoring me completely as he went through his lighting ritual, he continued. "So you're going to tell your buddy Kevin that R&D contractors have volunteered to fix up…whatever room the media will be in. They'll only do the back wall and about six feet of the ones on either side in time for the fund-raiser, but the kid doesn't have to know that. What I want is for the TV cameras to get a night-and-day difference between how things should be and how they are, so that when the chief is called up to say a few words, he'll be delivering one hell of a powerful subliminal message. Here's the chief, in front of a neat, clean wall surrounded by filth and squalor! The chief and the future of the state surrounded by its present. It's perfect,! I'd imagine even *you* can see that."

"Gee, I think so," I said, "But what if the contractors are able to get more—or less—done than you envision?"

C.C. looked at me with that expression of total contempt I'd grown so accustomed to seeing on his face when addressing anyone over whom he felt he had control. "Christ, Hardesty, does your mother dress you in the morning? Not that it's any of your business, but R&D Contractors just happens to be run by my wife's second cousin. He'll know exactly how much to get done by the fund-raiser, and he'll do it. Do I have to spell it out for you?"

I shook my head slowly. "I have to hand it to you, Mr. Carlson! I *never* would have thought of that subliminal thing. I'll bet Chief Rourke was impressed."

C.C. took a long puff on his cigar. "He will be. I'm running the P.R. end of this show, and I don't have to bother the chief with every little detail in advance. That's why he has an expert team of professionals like me to smooth the path for him. I told McNearny about it, and that's all I need to cover my ass."

He looked at me and raised his eyebrows. "Well, what the hell are you standing there for? You know what you have to do. So go do it."

And I did.

*   *   *

Kevin was of course thrilled to think that the shelter's dining room might be getting a badly needed renovation, and said he'd call R&D immediately. It never occurred to him that there might be a direct link between the offer and the conflict of interest issue. I felt rather guilty not letting him in on the other details, but C.C. was doing a great job of digging himself a nice deep hole, and I didn't want to do anything to keep him from burying himself in it.

I recognized, while driving home that evening, that I was really pretty ambivalent in my feelings—if that's not too strong a word—about Kevin. On the one hand, I readily admitted that I was attracted to the guy, and the little episode at the S.A.P.C. meeting didn't exactly detract from that. I hardly had visions of us settling down together and living happily ever after, but good sex is good sex. And nearly every time I started thinking about him, I somehow felt sorry for the guy. Just to be able to survive in that unimaginably dysfunctional family was cause for grudging respect.

On the other side of the coin, of course, there was the whole issue of the hypocrisy of allowing himself to be manipulated into a marriage I suspected was largely a showcase arrangement; to not have the guts Patrick, however screwed up *he* undoubtedly was, somehow found to get out. On the religion, I figured it wasn't my place to fault him—he quite obviously really did care about helping others, and if it took the form of borderline zealotry to enable him to survive and do what he had to do, so be it.

Bob called shortly after I got home to ask if I could come up to his apartment a little later in the evening. He'd mentioned several days before that he was planning to get together with the owners of the other burned out bars to see if they could do something together with the Bar Guild to try to shake the insurance companies off the fence, and they were coming over to his place around nine. Since what little information I had been able to get on Bob's behalf was apparently considerably more than any of them had as individuals, Bob thought they might like to hear it directly from me. I told him I'd be glad to.

A quick dinner and some TV, and it was time to head upstairs to Bob's.

The owners of all six of the burned out bars were there—the Dog Collar's owner was in jail, unable to make the million dollar bail. Some of them I knew, some I didn't. I told them everything I could without mentioning Tom or betraying my promise to him. When I'd finished, Mark Graser, owner of Hype, the first bar to have burned and apparently spokesman for the group looked around at the others, who nodded in apparent agreement to something I wasn't aware of.

"Dick," Mark said; "Bob had told us of everything you've done for him and, needless to say, he thinks pretty highly of you. You've been able to find out more than any one of us has individually, and what we need most is to all be on the same page when it comes to dealing with our insurance companies. We're all pretty financially strapped right now, but we were wondering if there might be some way we could hire you to act on all our behalves in finding out who's behind these fires. We know if we sit and wait for the police to do it, it'll be a long, long wait. And if we had one reliable source of information, it would save us a hell of a lot of time and duplication of effort. It would mean a lot to all of us."

I looked around at the group. "I really appreciate your offer, Mark…and guys…but you don't have to hire me to do anything. I'll be more than happy to pass on anything I can find out. Bob's probably told you I've got a really awkward job working with the P.R. firm hired to get Chief Rourke elected governor, but I just can't afford to give it up right now. However, because of this job, I just might be able to learn some things I couldn't have found out otherwise. When this campaign is over, I know damned well I'm going to be out of a job and I might have to come knocking on your doors, but by that time I hope they'll have nailed the guy behind the fires and you won't need me."

"Well, we'll sure as hell owe you," Mark said.

I made a mental note of that for future reference.

*   *   *

I had several meetings with Kevin in the next week—he was still kept incredibly busy trying to juggle his duties at the shelter with speaking engagements for the chief. As I'd expected, while C.C. got all the credit, I got all the work in preparations for the fund-raiser. Dunning calls to the media for coverage, press releases, a few human interest articles on the shelter and its good works, etc. The press releases all emphasized the fact that the event was for raising money for the shelter and that, coincidentally, the chief would be making a few remarks, but nobody was fooled as to its real purpose. C.C. and the chief's team lined up prominent potential contributors and urged attendance as a show of support for the chief. Formal invitations were sent out and would be checked at the door lest any homeless intrude on the festivities.

R&D Contractors arrived the Thursday before the event, much to Kevin's dismay. "They'll never get the room painted in time!" he told me, and I did not pass on the information that they weren't *supposed* to; that it was just a glorified photo op. Instead, I tried to reassure him that it really didn't matter, and that the important thing was that it would get done eventually. And I vowed to myself that if it *didn't*, that fact and the relationship between C.C. and his wife's second cousin would somehow be tipped to the media.

Sunday dinner would be over at 12:30—that would give us only an hour and a half to clean up from lunch and set up for the fund-raiser. McNearny had indicated that he would leave the details to Kevin and me as long as we kept him informed, and we decided to simply leave the room basically set up as it was. We were informed that about 200 people would be in attendance which would greatly overtax the kitchen's staff and equipment. While I'm sure C.C. and certain members of the chief's team—not to mention many of those corralled or coerced into attending—were thoroughly repulsed by the idea, we'd convinced McNearny that the food served should be basically the same as a typical lunch for the homeless; soup, sandwiches, milk, coffee, cake and, as a concession to the occasion, a non-alcoholic punch. Kevin had recruited extra volunteers for the kitchen staff.

*   *   *

The Sunday arrived. On C.C.'s explicit instructions, I had convinced Kevin to leave the scaffolding, tarps, and various paint cans exactly as they were, despite the inconvenience to the homeless in getting to the window between the kitchen and the dining room where the food was dispensed. A lectern—the one Kevin used as a pulpit in the shelter's makeshift chapel—was brought in for the chief's remarks, and strategically placed for maximum visual effect in contrasting the freshly painted wall with the drabness of the rest of the room. To spare the invited guests the inconvenience of sidestepping the painting equipment as the homeless were expected to do, tables were set up just inside the entrance for the food service and everything prepared in advance so that the kitchen could in effect be shut down before the fund-raiser began. For as little painting as had actually been done, the smell of fresh paint was nearly overpowering.

C.C. was there, of course, glad-handing all and sundry and making it clear that whatever success the event may have was totally due to his own tireless efforts. I was a bit surprised by the turnout, and by the representation from the media. I suspected it was due in part to the reporters' speculation as to whether the chief would be able to present himself as a real human being. For a man running for the office of governor of the state, he had been rarely seen in public other than under the most strictly controlled circumstances since the Dog Collar fire.

I noticed that, apart from the reporters and various media people, very few attendees took more than coffee or punch from the food provided. Had the sandwiches been caviar rather than tuna or ham salad, I'm sure there would have been more attention paid to the extraordinary work Kevin and his volunteers put into its preparation.

There was a stir when, about halfway through the scheduled time set for the event, the chief swept into the room accompanied by the rest of the family including Sue-Lynn and baby Sean. It did seem as though the chief were making a very serious effort to appear congenial, and I wondered if he may actually have taken McNearny up on his suggestion to hire a professional humanizer. Kevin greeted them all, as he had greeted everyone who came in and then, a few moments later, moved to the podium. The room settled down, and he began to speak.

Once again, Kevin surprised me. He thanked everyone for coming and then spoke about what the shelter meant to him and, most importantly, to the homeless people it served. He was warm, and sincere, and charming—qualities which, if possessed by his father, would have made his election to the governor's mansion a much easier task.

At last, he introduced his father, and a loud round of applause from the faithful and the turning on of lights for the TV cameras accompanied the chief to the podium. He and Kevin shook hands warmly, and then the chief did the unthinkable—he actually reached out and hugged his son; an act which not only surprised the hell out of me, but obviously out of Kevin, too.

Kevin left the podium and moved to the back of the room to join Sue-Lynn and the rest of the family.

The chief waited for silence, and then began: "A man's family...."

And at that point there was a tremendous explosion and the freshly painted wall dividing the kitchen from the dining room moved slowly forward into the room, disintegrating as it came.

CHAPTER 14

Impressive it certainly was. The Dog Collar fire it was not. The chief appeared on every newspaper front page and TV screen in the country somersaulting over the lectern, a look of complete shock on his face. He landed flat on his back on a table about three feet in front of the lectern and, apart from a few bruises and a badly shaken sense of control, was completely unscathed. There were several minor injuries among the others in the room, mostly cuts and bruises, and considerable initial panic, but little in the way of permanent damage either to the spectators or, it turned out, to the building itself. The wall which blew out had been an addition when the shelter took over and did not involve any real major structural elements. The cause of the blast was determined to have been the antiquated oven which Kevin had worked so frequently and diligently to repair; the odor of escaping gas completely overpowered by the paint fumes.

The overall result of the incident was a mixed bag. The chief got a lot more public exposure than he'd ever contemplated—though how or if it would actually affect his standing with the voters remained to be seen. Kevin received far more in spontaneous public donations in the wake of the explosion than the fund-raiser itself actually brought in. C.C. frantically tap danced himself away from any responsibility for anything—especially the all too obvious fact that had the entire room been either entirely painted as it should have been before the event, or left unpainted, someone would undoubtedly have noticed the leaking gas in time to prevent the explosion. He didn't even attempt to pass the blame on to me.

*   *   *

All in all, things eventually settled down and got back to whatever it was that passed for normal. There had been no more new bar fires—though the arson squad, as I heard through Tom, suspected the arsonist could merely be laying low for a while. They still had not conclusively proved or disproved whether it was the same arsonist in all seven fires: the basic elements were the same, but …. Tamasini, whose M.O. the arsonist had copied so faithfully in the six non-fatal fires, was questioned extensively and repeatedly, but could or would give no information that would advance the investigation. The gallon jar which held the gas for the Dog Collar fire was determined by exhaustive chemical analysis to have contained the jumbo olives served in most restaurants and bars.

The gay community slowly overcame much of its fear, and the bars began to fill up again. Bacchus' Lair reopened, and Bob and I decided to go out for dinner and take in the show. Neither of us had really been—or felt like being—out, other than to dinner, since the Dog Collar, but we both realized that our lives, however in disarray they might be, lay ahead of us, not in the past.

Arriving at Bacchus' Lair, we noted that the entrance had been widened to include three outward-opening doors. New occupancy limit signs were in evidence at the top and the bottom of the stairway. Emergency lights flanked the stairway and, in the bar itself a new emergency exit had been installed at the back of the hall leading to the rest rooms. A security guard was also in evidence.

Still, the place was not nearly as crowded as it had been prior to the fire. And I couldn't help but notice that several other people had adopted my preference for seats near the exits.

We'd just placed our drink order when T/T swept up to the table. Without a word, he leaned over and kissed Bob resoundingly on the cheek. "How 'ya doin', sugar?" T/T asked sincerely.

"I'm fine, thanks, Teddy. And thanks for the card. It meant a lot."

"You're more than welcome, darlin'," he said, then turned

to me. "And how are *you* doin', you hot hunk o' gorgeousness?"

"The check's in the mail, Teddy," I said, grinning. "But thanks for the vote of confidence. Do you have time for a drink?"

T/T shook his head. "Sorry, honey, but it's almost show time. But you give me a rain check, hear? Great show tonight. You just wait!" And with a squeeze to both Bob's and my shoulder, he moved off toward the stage.

Remembering my conversation with T/T at Griff's, I looked idly around the room and asked Bob: "You know Dave Lee, right?"

Bob nodded. "The manager?" he asked.

"Yeah. I don't think I've ever seen him."

Bob looked around then gave a small jerk of his head toward the bar, indicating a tall, dark-haired guy about 40, dressed all in black. "The guy at the end, talking to the bartender. I don't know him very well. He's a good manager, but he sort of keeps his distance."

"So I've heard," I said. "I still wonder who actually owns the place."

Bob thought a minute, then said: "Yeah. I honestly don't know. Rumors, of course, but I don't put much stock in them. If I was to guess, I'd say it's probably owned by some straight guy or group of straight businessmen who like the money a well run gay bar can bring in, but don't want to be identified as actually having anything to do with it."

"Mmmmm," I said. "Makes sense. Still, I'm curious."

Bob grinned at me: "See? You should have taken up the offer the other night. You'd make a great private detective!"

Before I had a chance to respond, the lights dimmed, the music blared, and the show started.

T/T was mostly right. It was a good show, but not great. Nobody new—that cute redhead with more looks than talent was back, and quite a bit better than I'd remembered. T/T was terrific, of course—he had real talent and the audience loved him. I wondered where he might have been able to go in show business if he hadn't opted for drag.

During the intermission, several guys came over to Bob to offer their condolences on Ramón's death. I knew they were sincere and meant well, but I could also see how close to the surface of Bob's emotions Ramón's death still was.

The second half of the show was highlighted by the cute redhead's surprisingly accurate lip synch to Jeanette MacDonald's "San Francisco;" Jeanette would have been proud. And finally it was time for Judy.

"Ladies and Gentleman," the offstage voice announced: "Miss Judy Garland!" There was the usual enthusiastic applause as the curtains opened, then the usual utter silence as Judy stepped forward and raised her mike. Even before she opened her mouth, I sensed something...well, *different*, but had no idea what it was. The spot narrowed to just her face, and she began to sing "I'm Always Chasing Rainbows" and I realized what the difference was...she was actually looking at the audience! No stares, of course, but little flickers from face to face. A small thing, true, but this was the first time she'd even seemed aware that there was anybody out there in the dark. I don't know if I was the only one to notice. She got the usual thunderous ovation, of course, and she actually smiled and gave a little nod of recognition. She then went into "Come Rain or Come Shine," and it struck me that while her choices weren't nearly so...well...sad...as when Chris and I saw her the last time, she wasn't doing any of the really upbeat stuff, either.

Her last number was "I Can't Give You Anything But Love," and for the first time her eyes wandered over to our table. Dark as it was in the room, I felt her eyes sweep past my own, and then return, for just an instant, and there was the slightest hint of a smile. My imagination, probably. But somehow I didn't think so.

And at the end of the song, and her set, the customary standing ovation. And then she was gone.

Bob and I finished our drinks, agreeing that we had both missed not being out among the crowd, and vowing to do it on a regular basis. We moved up to the bar for a nightcap and to shoot the shit with some guys we both knew.

It was nearly one o'clock when I got home. The red light was flashing on my answering machine. I pressed "Listen" and heard Kevin's obviously stressed voice:

"Dick. This is Kevin. Please call me the minute you get this. I'm at the shelter, and I'll wait here until I hear from you. It's very important!"

Curious, but not really expecting him to still be there at that time of night, I dialed the shelter's number. The phone was picked up on the first ring. "Salvation's Door."

I recognized the voice. "Kevin?" I said. "This is Dick. I just got in. What's the problem?"

"Patrick's back," he said.

*   *   *

I arrived at the all-night diner about five minutes before Kevin and ordered a pot of coffee with two cups. We'd agreed to meet there as an alternative to my coming to the shelter, which was locked down for the night, or Kevin's coming to my place, which I did not even suggest for a number of reasons.

I was seated in a booth in a far corner of the nearly empty diner, nursing my coffee, when Kevin came in. He looked tired and understandably distraught. Sliding into the bench opposite me, he got right down to business.

"What am I going to do, Dick? What am I going to do?" he asked.

"Well, before we go into that," I said, "tell me exactly what happened."

Kevin started to pour himself a cup of coffee and then apparently decided against it, pushing the cup aside. "The day after the explosion," he said, "I got a message from one of the volunteers that I had had a call from somebody named 'Pat.' I was getting all sorts of calls, of course, and didn't think a thing of it—there are lots of 'Pat's, both male and female, and I just let it pass. A few days later there was another message, which came in to the shelter while Sue-Lynn and I were in Evertston meeting with a group of my father's supporters. Again it didn't register. And whoever called didn't leave a number where I could have called back."

He reached for the coffee carafe and poured half a cup, then poured so much sugar in it I thought the spoon would be able to stand up by itself.

"Then tonight, I was just going up to my office for my prayers and meditation when I happened to walk past the phone. It rang, and when I picked up...I recognized his voice immediately. 'How's it going, little brother?' he asked. Patrick is 12 minutes older than I am; nobody else would know that. I was so nervous I couldn't say anything for a minute, and I finally asked him where he was. 'Around,' he said." Kevin looked at me with an expression of anguish. "He wouldn't tell me where he was, but I know he's here in the city somewhere."

"How can you be sure?" I asked.

Kevin shook his head. "I just know," he said, " I *felt* it. Unless you have an identical twin, you couldn't understand what I mean, but..." he looked into his coffee. I sensed there was something more he wasn't saying.

"But...?" I prompted.

Kevin gave a deep sigh and a shrug. "...we always just *knew* things about each other; ever since we were babies. And now I'm certain he's here, and that he's been here for months!"

I shook my head, trying to follow what he was saying. He anticipated my next question without waiting for me to ask it.

"I've had this same feeling several times in the past couple of months, but I refused to pay attention to it. Twice, people I know mentioned having seen me around town in places that I knew I couldn't have been at the time! It didn't register —probably because I didn't *want* it to register. I just thought they were mistaken. Again, it never occurred to me that Patrick might be back—it just didn't. It's been so long now."

"And have you told anybody about this?" I asked.

"Nobody," he said. "But I know Patrick is back and that he's going to do whatever he can to destroy my father's career."

I thought a good long time before saying: "You can't jump to that conclusion, Kev. If he wanted to do that, all he would have to do is call the media—or any of your father's political enemies."

Kevin gave a wry little smile. "Oh, no. No," he said, "you don't know Patrick. You have no idea of how evil he is. He called me for a reason, and he is out to do something terrible and I have no idea of what it is or how to prevent it." His eyes locked on mine. "And you have no idea of what this is doing to me—what it has done to me all these years. Patrick is evil. Truly evil, and it's as though the devil himself had created him to destroy me and my entire family. And still..." he bit his lower lip and shook his head slowly back and forth..."... and still, he is my brother and I love him and I miss him. How can I love him? How?"

I had no idea what to say. Kevin was obviously in a place I had no desire ever to go. I felt tremendously sorry for him in spite of my resolve not to get involved with him in any way.

Kevin was still staring at me, obviously desperate for help, or advice, or something. Suddenly, to my total surprise, he reached across the table and took my hand. "Can I spend the night at your house, Dick?" he asked.

I was sure the hell glad I was sitting down, because if I wasn't, my legs might have given out from under me. "Kev," I said, "I...I don't think that's a very good idea."

"Please, Dick! I can't go home; it's much too late. I often stay over at the shelter, but I just can't go back there tonight. What if Patrick were to call again? I could go to a hotel, of course, but...."

I was mildly surprised to realize he was still holding my hand, and more than a little pissed at myself when I felt myself starting to get aroused. *Jesus, Hardesty! Get a grip!*

Reluctantly, and with my better judgment yelling *Don't do it!* I said: "Okay, Kev. If you're sure. I've got a guest bedroom you can use."

As if suddenly realizing himself that he still held my hand, he released it quickly and said: "Thanks."

We left the restaurant, and I said: "I'll drive if you want." But Kevin shook his head.

"That's okay," he said. "I'll take my own car and follow you."

*   *   *

All the way home, checking the rear-view mirror several times to make sure Kevin was still behind me, my mind was working overtime on several levels at once.

Stupid move, Hardesty!

What was Patrick up to? Why would he come back after so many years? Well, that part was fairly obvious—the chief's bid for governor had been mentioned to one degree or another across the country—it was pay back time.

You're going to regret this!

But if he was coming back to ruin his father's chance for governor, why *didn't* he just go public with his whole story? That would pretty much accomplish what he wanted. Could Kevin be right about Patrick having some other, sinister motive or motives? And what in hell could they possibly be? If coming back was going to cut off his source of income, I'd imagine whatever it was would have to be pretty important to him.

He does suck a mean cock! JEEZUS, HARDESTY!!

As we approached my apartment building, I noticed a parking place about halfway up the block and slowed to open the window and motion to Kevin to take it. Then I pulled into the building's garage and walked back to the street to meet him.

I noticed it was just after 3:30 when we entered my apartment, and realized I was completely exhausted. I showed Kevin to the guest bedroom, which was still cluttered with Chris's boxes. He shook my hand and thanked me again, and I went into my own room, where I undressed, climbed under the covers, and immediately fell into a very deep sleep.

I felt Chris coming to bed, and I rolled over and slipped my arms around him without bothering to wake up. He snuggled closer, and we just held one another. He put his head against my chest, and he must have been cold, because I could feel him shivering. I just pulled him closer, and it felt warm and comfortable and the way it should always be....

* * *

I awoke with a start. A bar of sunlight stretched across the bed from the partially open curtains. Chris was...

Chris?

I jumped out of bed, grabbed my robe from behind the door, and went directly to the guest bedroom. The door was open, the bed unmade, but no sign of Kevin. I checked the bathroom, then went into the kitchen. On the counter was a note:

Dick: Many thanks for your hospitality. Have to get to the shelter for morning services. Kevin

I do not have a closet full of dunce caps. I can occasionally complete an entire crossword puzzle all by myself, and I can dress myself without assistance when necessary. But when it came to Kevin and the clan Rourke, I honestly hadn't a clue. Either Kevin knew damned well what little game he was playing and what the rules were, or he was one *very* strange young man. And I tended to opt for the latter.

For some reason, I was reminded of the kid I took home while I was still in college. He was hot as hell, but all he wanted to do was to masturbate using my tennis shoes. Fine for him, but sort of zilch for me. I actually went home with him a second time because I simply couldn't believe the first. Tennis shoes: 2; Hardesty: 0.

One thing was for sure, with Patrick back on the scene, things were going to get a lot more interesting. And I wanted to talk to Patrick very badly.

* * *

Bob called around 9:30 wanting to know if I wanted to join him for brunch. He'd gotten a call from an old friend who had recently moved back to town, and whom he thought I might like to meet. Hey, I'm not above a little matchmaking, so I agreed.

We met Don at Rasputin's. Don Yosling, Bob had informed me on the way to the restaurant, was now a forensic pathologist for the state, but had been Bob's roommate at college. Don's lover of 15 years had recently died, and Bob thought it would be a good idea for the three of us to join up and take a little walk down the path back to the real world together.

Don turned out to be a really nice guy, about ten years older than I, but quite handsome in a "grows-on-you" kind of way. He was very soft spoken, but had a sharp, wry sense of humor. He was also quite shy, which both surprised and pleased me a bit. I've always had a soft spot for shy guys, and while he was very subtle about it, I caught him looking at me a couple of times and got a definite vibe or two.

By mutual unspoken agreement, none of us mentioned our ex's and I for one had a really good, relaxed time. And I was very much aware how much I really needed a time like that.

When Don mentioned his car was in the shop, Bob and I volunteered to give him a ride home. Despite his protestations of not wanting to bother us and the ready availability of public transportation, we convinced him.

It was nearly 2:30 by the time we left Rasputin's and Bob, looking at his watch, said: "Damn! Dick, would you mind dropping me off at the apartment? It's right on the way, and I completely forgot that there's a Bar Guild meeting at 4!"

Don, who was sitting in the back seat, said: "I can just catch a bus from your place, then. It's right on my line."

"Hey, it's no problem," I said. "Don't worry about it. It's really good just to get out!"

We dropped Bob off at the apartment and Don got into the front seat beside me. Don and Bob agreed to call one another during the week, and Bob retreated into the building.

"You're sure you don't mind running me all the way home?"

Don asked.

"My pleasure," I said, and got the odd sensation that I really meant it. I realized that other than that whatever-it-was-you-could-call-it romp with Kevin at the hotel, I hadn't had sex in what seemed like several eternities. Of course, to a Scorpio, two days without sex is an eternity. Not that I assumed that was what was going to happen with Don, but if he did show any interest, I certainly wouldn't mind.

On the way, we covered a lot of conversational ground, including the upcoming elections. Either I or Bob had mentioned at brunch about my working with the chief's P.R. team and while Don was much too polite to say anything, I did get a quizzical look. He made it quite clear that his opinion of the chief pretty well paralleled my own, and he began asking a few questions about the chief's private life—about which very little was still actually known by the general public. Without going into too much detail, I mentioned the various family members and the fact that Kevin's identical twin Patrick had disappeared on a hunting trip. He appeared very interested, and wanted to know where and how Patrick had disappeared.

"Up near Neelyville, from what I understand," I said. "He apparently fell from a cliff into the river, which was in flood stage. His body was never found," I added, obviously not mentioning why.

Don nodded. "That's too bad. I remember hearing about it when it happened. The Oak's a mean river when it floods And didn't it just come out that…Kevin?…was gay?"

"Patrick was gay, yes. Kevin's married and therefore couldn't possibly be…one of *those*," I said, grinning.

Don returned the grin. "Ah, Patrick, yes…sorry. Anyway, it's not unusual for bodies not to be retrieved in circumstances like that. Sometimes they might turn up later downstream somewhere. But more often than not, they're never found. A real shame for the families."

We arrived at Don's apartment and I pulled up into an empty space not far from the front door.

"Could I offer you a drink for having dragged you all the way out here?" Don asked.

"Sure," I said. "Why not?"

Don's apartment was nice, and rather reminded me of mine in that it looked a little sparse—his from just having moved in, mine from Chris's just having moved out. Don fixed our drinks and we sat together on his large, comfortable sofa, talking. But it soon became quite evident to both of us where the conversation was going.

Finally, Don took the initiative. "So what do you think of older men?" he asked.

"Like who?" I asked.

He smiled. "Spoken like a true diplomat," he said. "Like me, for example."

"Shit!" I said. "Ask me when you get there."

"Well," he said, "it does matter to a lot of guys. Once you're past 30, you're pond scum."

"A lot of guys are idiots," I said. "I go to bed with what's inside a person, not what's outside. And if you ask me, you're pretty hot either way."

"Let's find out," he said.

And we did.

*   *   *

Don had given up smoking and there were no ashtrays evident in the bedroom, so I forced myself not to ask for one and abstained. The sex, like the brunch, was just exactly what I needed, and even more enjoyable.

"Okay for an old guy?" he asked.

"You give me that 'old guy' routine one more time and I'll smother you with this pillow," I said. "And any time you want to start a sex school for some of these younger twinks, you could make a fortune."

We lay side by side quietly for a while and Don said: "I owe you, Dick. This is my first time since...in a long time. It's nice to know it can still be good."

"I know exactly what you mean," I said. I couldn't really count the time with Kevin, since he did all the work and he wouldn't let me return the favor.

"I'd like it if we might get to be friends," Don said. "And you don't have to worry about me trying to latch on to you. I'm nowhere near even *thinking* about the possibility of another relationship. But an occasional fuck with a friend would sure be great."

"You took the words right out of my mouth," I said, and Don reached over and took my hand, moving it down to his crotch.

"Then let me put something back in there," he said.

CHAPTER 15

Kevin had called the office before I got there Monday morning and left a message for me to call. I'd been able to pretty well avoid thinking about Kevin for much of Sunday, but seeing his message pulled me right back in. I wasn't sure whether I hoped he'd had another call from Patrick, or if I hoped he hadn't.

"Kev," I said when I heard his voice on the phone. "What's up? Any more…calls?"

"Two," he said. "Can you come over? We have to talk."

"Sure," I said. "I'll be over as soon as I can."

C.C. entered the office just as I was hanging up the phone. He'd been pretty subdued since the shelter explosion, and while he was still all business, some of the arrogant bluster seemed to be missing. But there was still enough of the old C.C. for him to manage to pretend I didn't exist. He marched past me without a word and went into his office.

Without bothering to notify C.C., I told the secretary I'd be at the shelter, and left.

* * *

Workmen had rebuilt the blown out wall, and the dining room had been completely repainted; it looked good. R&D Contractors had mysteriously gone from the scene, the insurance company preferring to recommend another firm for the work. The kitchen was still a work in progress, but it would have all new appliances and a larger service capacity. Kevin was overseeing the installation of the new sinks and countertops when I arrived, and he quickly excused himself and led me upstairs to his office.

There were a few very large cracks in the wall, some missing tiles in the ceiling, and some obviously warped floorboards from the force of the explosion in the kitchen below. The bulletin board was on the floor, propped against the cracked wall, and the photo of Kevin, Sue-Lynn and Sean had lost its glass. The door to the office had been removed, I assumed because the door frame had probably shifted.

We took our customary seats, but with Kevin turning his chair slightly so as better to keep an eye on the doorway, should someone come up the stairs. Leaning forward, he said in a low semi whisper: "Twice. Patrick called twice. Once yesterday morning, just after services and once last night, just before I began my prayers and meditation. I think he may have called once after that, but the phone downstairs is not to be answered after 9:30 at night. It is for incoming calls only because it is in the hallway and could easily be abused by some of our flock. The only outgoing phone is the one on my desk. And I will let nothing disturb my prayers and meditation."

"And what did he have to say?" I asked.

Kevin looked flustered and embarrassed. "It was disgusting," he said. "He said he was calling right while he was being…while he was…engaging in a disgusting and depraved sex act! He was laughing and making disgusting…noises. 'You don't know what you're missing, little brother,' he said. I wanted to hang up, but I couldn't. Finally, he started breathing heavily and said 'Too close to talk now. I'll call you back!"

I didn't say a word. What in hell could I say? But Kevin was so obviously distraught, I felt really sorry for him.

"And the second call?" I asked, hoping for Kevin's sake it wasn't a repeat of the first.

"As I said, it was just before nine. I'd just been up to the dormitories talking with the night attendants, and had come down to lock the front doors. Just as I passed the phone, it rang. Normally, I would not have answered it, but somehow I knew who it was."

Kevin had his head bowed down, and his hands were clasped as if in prayer, but he wasn't praying.

He raised his head up just enough to look at me. "He was very nice," Kevin said, his voice softer and reflexive. "He didn't even mention the earlier call, and I simply couldn't. He asked how I was, and how Sue-Lynn and the baby were doing, and that he'd heard of the explosion and was glad no one was hurt, and he sounded as though he really, really meant it. We talked just like brothers. He was so normal and happy and….."I noticed that his eyes were misting, and he quickly wiped at them with the back of his hand. "And do you know what, Dick?" he asked. I shook my head. "That hurt me as much as the first call had. *That* was my brother! *That* was the Patrick I wanted—that my parents wanted."

"Did you ask him where he was?" I asked.

"Yes, but he wouldn't tell me. He's here in the city, though. I could *feel* it. He did say he had a very good job that he liked a lot, but didn't say what it was or where. I told him I wanted to see him, but he said no. 'We'll see each other soon enough,' he said. 'I don't think you're ready yet.' I asked him what he meant by that, but he just said 'I've got to go, little brother. I'll call again soon.' And he hung up. I called the operator to see if she could trace the call, but she said she couldn't."

I thought in silence for a good long minute, with Kevin's eyes on my face, waiting for me to say something.

"The next time he calls," I said, "ask him if he would be willing to meet with me. Tell him I won't betray him to anyone, but that I really want to hear his side of the story. Maybe I can help."

Kevin shook his head. "I don't think that's a good idea, Dick," he said. "Patrick is playing with me. I know that. Those two calls…he knew exactly what he was doing in both of them. The devil lures with honey, and you have no idea of the power of evil."

This time it was me who reached out for his hand. He looked truly startled and almost pulled back. I only touched him in a brief, reassuring pat, then withdrew. "Kevin, you have got to get to the bottom of this thing. We have to find out exactly what

Patrick is up to and what he hopes to achieve. I suspect you're right that his ultimate goal is to ruin your father's chances for election. But he hasn't done anything yet, and we won't know for sure until we talk to him. You're under too much pressure as it is; I can be a little more objective. Will you do this for me? When he calls again, will you try to find out if he really is in the city and if he will meet with me?"

Kevin sighed and searched my face with his eyes. Then he nodded.

At that moment, the phone rang.

Kevin jumped up from his chair and reached quickly forward over the desk to get to the phone. "Salvation's Door," he said. There was a pause, and I could see him literally sag as his muscles relaxed. "Yes," he said. "It arrived this morning. And I want to thank you for your wonderful generosity. It will mean so much to our flock. Yes. Thank you again. May God bless you. Good bye."

Kevin hung up the phone, turned, shrugged, and sighed. He was about to sit down again when a voice called from the bottom of the stairs: "Reverend Rourke? Could you come down to the kitchen, please?"

"Yes…yes, I'll be right there." He turned again to me with a sad little smile. "We never do seem to finish what we start, do we, Dick?"

"No, Kev, " I said, "we don't." *No, Kev,* I thought, *we don't.*

We walked down the stairs together, and just as Kevin was moving into the dining room, I stopped him. "You'll ask, right?"

Kevin nodded, and I left.

* * *

I had tried to keep in regular contact with Tom, but we kept playing telephone tag and didn't really have a chance to talk in person all that much. I did manage to reach him Monday evening and we talked briefly There had been a minor fire at Ruth's, a lesbian bar, but it happened in the early afternoon and was quickly traced to an electrical problem. The arson squad had been informed of it, but hadn't been involved at all.

Knowing that the gallon jar used in the Dog Collar fire originally held jumbo olives wasn't as big a clue as they had hoped: there were just too many bars and restaurants in the city—even within a two mile radius of the Dog Collar. Empty gallon jars of that kind were in pretty big demand for a lot of storage uses, and it was almost impossible for those places which did not break up their glass containers after use to keep track of what happened to them. One bartender at a straight restaurant was found to have had a previous arson arrest and was questioned extensively, but had what proved to be a watertight alibi for the night of the fire.

Gas stations were checked to see if anyone had been seen filling or attempting to fill a gallon glass jar but, since it was a violation of state law to sell gasoline in any container other than red cans meeting state regulations, if anyone *had* seen...or sold gas to...someone filling up a gallon glass jar, they weren't going to admit to it.

I thanked Tom and invited him to go out for dinner the following Saturday. He agreed.

On Wednesday, Don Yosling, Bob, and I got together for an early dinner, where I passed on the information Tom had given me. After dinner, Don and I went to my place for a little horizontal recreation. We both seemed to realize we had lucked out in finding a sex partner with no danger of the relationship going any further for either one of us.

Thursday came, and still no word from Kevin. I knew he had been out of town on speaking assignments both Tuesday and Wednesday, but still....

The chief, with nothing substantial going on in the Dog Collar investigation and therefore no valid reason to remain holed up in his office, was forced to begin accepting carefully monitored and scripted public appearances, with the primary emphasis on "appearances" and as little "public" as could be gotten away with. That wouldn't take much pressure off Kevin, of course, since he had in fact become the designated human contact in the chief's campaign.

I'd just finished dinner Thursday night and debating whether the mountain of dirty dishes in the sink and stacked on the counters really needed attention when the phone rang. It was Kevin.

"He called?" I asked, without even saying 'hello.'

"Yes," Kevin said, "just now."

"And?"

"And he wouldn't agree to meeting you…or me. He asked me why you were 'butting in,' as he put it, and what you wanted and how I knew I could trust you and then he started going off again."

I had an idea what he meant, but wanted to be sure. "How so 'going off'?" I asked. "Exactly what did he say?"

Kevin hesitated. "When he first started talking, he was fine, but when I started answering his questions about you he started…well…I really don't feel comfortable talking about this, Dick. It was disgusting and perverted and he made all sorts of sickening accusations about…"

"About…?" I prompted.

"You…and me." He paused again. "And I fell right into his trap—I found myself defending myself and denying his accusations and trying to reason with him, and…"

Another long pause, until at last I had to say: "Are you still there?"

"Yes," he said. "I'm still here. And finally I asked him again to please at least talk with you, and assured him that he would find you as trustworthy as I did, and then he said something really strange, which I still don't understand."

"What was that?" I asked.

"He said 'Oh, I know who…'" Kevin paused "…he…is.'"

I didn't miss the hesitation. "Did he use the word 'he'?"

I could almost hear him blush. "No," he said.

"Exactly what did he say, Kev? It might be important."

"I don't know if I can even say it, Dick…it was so ugly and

perverted."

"Come on, Kev," I said, a little impatiently. "It's just me and you. Exactly what did he say?". There was another hesitation and then Kevin blurted it out. "He said: 'I know who your boyfriend is.' What a disgusting thing to imply! Please don't be insulted! But how could he know who you are?"

I wondered exactly the same thing. "He probably just said that to get you upset," I said. "He might conceivably have found out that I work for C.C. and your father," I said, grasping at straws. "But more than likely he just said it to shake you...which apparently it did. I can assure you, if I had ever seen Patrick, I'd know it. Did he say anything else?"

"No, not really. He kept switching back and forth between being calm and conversational in one breath to being blasphemous and unspeakably perverted in the next. I hate to say it, Dick, but I truly suspect my brother is possessed by the Devil himself. You cannot imagine what filth he used when he talked about...us."

Yes, in fact I *could* imagine.

"So how did the conversation end?" I asked.

"He said it was time for him to go and...engage in his sexual perversions...and that he would call again soon. I don't know how much longer I can deal with this, Dick. I really don't. I have prayed, and prayed, and..."

I really empathized with the guy, but couldn't let him fall apart now. "Listen to me, Kev," I said. "I can imagine how hard this is for you—I really can." I searched for something to say that might mean something to him. Feeling just a little bit hypocritical, I said: "You have the power of your faith to protect you. Patrick can't harm you if you don't let him. If he is trying to shake you, don't let him. Don't let him win."

There was a long pause, and then a sigh. "You're right, of course," he said. "Thank you, Dick. You have no idea what your friendship means to me. But now I have to go to my prayers and meditation. Thank you again, and God bless you."

"Good bye, Kev," I said, and hung up.

*   *   *

Well, now I felt like a *real* shit. Kevin Rourke—closeted, bigoted, narrow-minded, stupifyingly uptight Kevin Rourke—considered me a friend! Me, who was out to do everything I could to keep his father from being elected governor. And the pathetic thing was I guessed from his standpoint, I *was* a friend—as I'd said before, I somehow felt in my bones that Kevin did not have many…if any…actual friends. Dominated by his father, stuck in a marriage I don't think even he could convince himself that he wanted. Living his entire life trying to be what others expected him to be. Our lifestyles could not conceivably be further apart. But he considered me his friend, and that made me very, strangely, sad.

And again, when it came right down to it, I felt a great deal of empathy for the poor guy. I could only imagine what he'd had to go through in his life. And I couldn't help but feel some respect for his ability to carry all that mental, emotional, and psychological baggage and still survive. Against all my better judgment, I guess I really did like the guy.

And Patrick. Why was I so intrigued with Patrick? The whole thing was none of my damned business. Leave Patrick to his own devices and let him bring the chief down on his own. That anyone could be as evil as Kevin painted his brother was hard to believe, until you looked at the whole dysfunctional mess of a family. And then the fact that Patrick might be as fucked up in one direction as Kevin was in the other wasn't that hard to accept. I just knew I had to know more about Patrick's side of the story.

Dick Hardesty: Collector of Lost Souls, I thought.

Deciding the dishes could wait a while longer, I had another cigarette and went to bed.

*   *   *

My work at the office had settled into a soporific routine. An endless string of press releases, press kits, head shots, a barrage of P.R. materials following every announced endorse-ment by some group or organization. A big to-do over the amazing and, from the chief's camp's ecstatic response, supposedly totally unexpected support of the National Rifle Association; the Christians for Democracy; the American Rights Foundation; Families for Justice, and other equally open minded organizations. Each endorsement was ranked right up there with the Second Coming in importance to the campaign, and heralded as such.

McNearny played puppeteer to Kevin's increasingly frenetic marionette as more and more time was demanded of him. Sean had caught a bad cold on one of the day trips with his mother and father, so Sue-Lynn, at least, was able to take some time out to care for the baby, while Kevin continued his endless string of speeches. He had, however, asserted himself to the point of gaining a grudging concession that he would not be scheduled for engagements from Friday evening through Sunday noon. I think even McNearny had some vague idea of how hard he was pushing and didn't want to risk losing Kevin altogether.

Kevin called me at home Saturday morning. He sounded a little tired, and more than a little depressed.

"I know it's the weekend, Dick, and I really shouldn't be bothering you at home, but do you suppose we might get together for a few minutes? For coffee, maybe?"

I could tell from his tone of voice that it didn't involve more calls from Patrick, and realized that he probably just wanted someone to talk to. Hey, I was his friend, right? Ah, well, fuck the 'no mixing business and pleasure.' It might not necessarily be a pleasure, but I figured I owed him, somehow.

There was the laundry to do, and groceries to buy, and that damned sink full of dishes, but....

"Sure, Kev," I said. "Do you want me to come to the shelter?"

"No," he said. "If I stay here, I'll feel like I have to work. The staff can handle lunch. I just need to relax for a little while. What's that coffee shop on the river...the one with the big windows?"

"Everly's?"

"Yes; that's the one. Would that be all right?"

"That will be fine," I said. "In about half an hour?"

*   *   *

On the way to the diner, I once again had a little heart-to-heart with myself, wondering what I really thought I was doing. Did I really want to get involved with Kevin on a personal level? I was reminded of one of my favorite bits of graffiti: on a bathroom wall in one of bars someone had written: "Tony's a SLUT!" and under it someone else had added "Yes, but he can suck a golf ball through a garden hose!"

Was I letting my memories of Kevin's oral abilities sway my thinking? It wouldn't be the first time my crotch had run away with my head. But I rationalized that while another round or two in the sack with Kevin would be interesting indeed, my main attraction was in finding out more about Patrick and what he had in the back of his mind. And the only way I was going to get to Patrick would be through Kevin.

*   *   *

Kevin was standing in front of Everly's when I got there, and we went in and found a table by the windows overlooking the river. Kevin ordered coffee and I opted for coffee and a piece of banana creme pie I'd noticed in the bakery case when we walked in.

"So," I asked as the waitress moved away to get my pie, "how are you doing?"

Kevin smiled and shrugged. "Okay, I guess. I'm used to talking in front of groups of people," he said, "but I much prefer to talk about the Lord and Salvation than about the current governor's shortcomings—though there are a lot of them," he hastened to add, almost as though he were afraid his father or McNearny might be listening.

I couldn't resist asking: "Tell me, Kev, what do you do for fun?"

He looked at me as though the question had never been asked him before. And it occurred to me that possibly it never had.

He actually looked confused and I could tell he had to think hard before answering."I read the Bible," he said. "And I really enjoy my work at the shelter—helping people brings me real joy." He subconsciously played his tongue against the inside corner of his lower lip. "I…uh…I enjoy playing the piano, and…" for some strange reason he actually blushed "…and singing, when no one is around. And playing with Sean, of course. I can't wait until he gets big enough for us to really do things together."

"No sports?" I asked.

Kevin thought a moment, then shook his head. "I'm afraid I really don't have the time," he said. "How about you?"

The waitress brought my pie, and I scooped up a large fork full before replying. "I boxed some in high school and college," I said.

"Were you any good?" Kevin asked.

"Well, I did make Golden Gloves. But after I got my nose broken the third time, I decided I'd better hang up the gloves for good."

Kevin stared at my nose. "It doesn't look like it's been broken."

"The fates were kind," I answered. "But I can see it when I look. And I really do enjoy water-skiing. A friend of our…" *oh, oh* "…a friend of mine has a cottage on Lake Verde and I used to spend a lot of time up there."

Kevin smiled wistfully. "I've always wanted to go water skiing," he said. "But my father always emphasized what he considered the more 'manly' sports. Patrick and I both hated them. Especially hunting…." His eyes suddenly dropped and he became very quiet.

"Nothing further from Patrick?" I asked and immediately regretted the insensitivity of the question.

Kevin took a sip of his coffee and put it back on the saucer, shaking his head. "No," he said. "It's like waiting for the other shoe to drop."

"I gather you haven't told your father?"

Kevin once again looked shocked. "Oh, my heavens, no! The only one I've told is you." He looked at me. "*You* haven't told anyone, have you?"

"Of course not, Kev. I made you a promise and I'll keep it." As I said it, I sincerely hoped I meant it.

One thing I have never really learned to do, and that is to leave well enough alone. I still had an awful lot of questions about Patrick, and Kevin was the only one who could even partially answer them.

"Kev," I began, "I hope you won't mind my asking these things, but the more I know about Patrick, the better I…we… might be able to know what he'd planning to do next."

Kevin responded with a noncommittal shrug. "Go ahead," he said.

The waitress appeared to ask if we needed anything else, and when we said "No" in unison, she placed the check on the table and went away. I used the time to try to formulate my questions in a way to elicit the most information without getting Kevin too upset.

"Tell me more about you and Patrick as kids," I said.

Kevin looked into his coffee cup and, seeing it was empty, pushed it toward the center of the table and leaned back into the booth.

"Patrick was born 12 minutes before I was," he began. "I think I told you that. He always made a big thing of his being the 'older' brother, and when we were younger—before he began to change—he always was the leader, and he always tried to protect me from things. I was always shy, Patrick always outgoing. When our parents would discipline us, Patrick was always more concerned for how I reacted than for himself. I looked up to him. Even then our being identical twins was more a matter of physical appearance than in character."

Kevin was quiet for a minute, looking out the window at a barge moving up the river. At last he looked back toward me, almost as if he was surprised to see me there.

"But then as we got older, things began to change," he went on. "Our parents, as I've said, were very strict. My father, especially, had a firm vision of what kind of adults Patrick and I should be, and his methods were…rather stern. Patrick rebelled at every turn, whereas I respected my parents' wishes even when I didn't agree with them. We were children, after all, and it was not our place to question. And Patrick increasingly resented me for not standing up to my parents, as he did. And, of course, that only made it all the worse for him; he saw himself as defending both of us, yet the punishment increasingly fell upon him. And for whatever reason, I could never defend him as he always defended me." He stared back out the window for another long moment, and then said softly: "I think Patrick felt I betrayed him. And sometimes I feel he was right."

He suddenly looked at me quickly, then sat up and reached for the check. "I really should be getting back, Dick," he said, a little briskly. "I really appreciate your coming out and meeting me. I did need the break."

Without waiting for any response from me, he stood up, reached into his wallet for some dollar bills, and put them under his saucer in the center of the table. It was as if he couldn't wait to leave.

And without a word I got up and followed him to the cashier's desk.

"Let me get that, Kev," I said, indicating the check in his hand, but he waved me off.

"No, no," he said. "It was I who dragged you out on your day off. It's the least I can do."

We left the diner without another word, shook hands in the parking lot and exchanged goodbyes, and that was it. Ten minutes, tops.

As I drove home, one thought kept recurring: *Kevin Rourke, you are one fucked up young man!*

*   *   *

I had three messages waiting for me when I got home: one from Chris asking me to call him, one from Tom to confirm our dinner for that night, and one from Don, asking if I had plans for the evening and if I'd like to go to dinner if I didn't. It had occurred to me that Don and Tom might get along quite well together, so I returned Tom's call first, asking if he minded if Don came with us. Tom was all for it, and I was a bit surprised when he suggested Rasputin's. Tom was obviously taking a few bold steps outside the closet.

I next called Don and invited him to join us, and he agreed. We all arranged to meet at Rasputin's at 8.

Chris, when I reached him, wanted me to ship out another couple of boxes of his things. He was settling in to his new apartment, still loved his job, and was apparently having a hell of a good time. I got the impression he might be seeing someone, but didn't ask, and he didn't volunteer any information.

Bob called a little later in the day, and I asked him if he'd like to join the group for dinner. He had other plans, but said he might be at Bacchus' Lair for the last show, if we felt like going over. I thought Bacchus' Lair might be just a tad too much for Tom's blood, but told Bob I'd suggest it to the others and see what they thought.

*   *   *

Dinner was very pleasant, and I had vastly underestimated the fact that Tom and Don might like one another: they hit it off immediately and the electricity between them could have lit up a room. Still, they both did their best not to ignore me completely. The only news Tom had on the fire(s) was that an unconfirmed rumor in the department was that a confidential file on Tamasini's M.O. had been stolen from the chief's office about two weeks before the first of the bar fires.

When, after dinner, I asked if Don and Tom might want to

go to Bacchus' Lair, there was a pregnant pause and a from-the-second-balcony exchange of glances between the two before Tom begged off, saying he had to be up early on Sunday, and Don saying that he, too, was suddenly very tired and thought maybe we should call it a night. *Uh-huh. Sure, guys.*

We left Rasputin's around 10:45 and I made a specific point, after bidding Tom and Don good night, of heading directly for my car and not looking back. I wouldn't have been surprised, if I had, to see the two of them stripping each other right there in the street.

I debated on just going home, but then thought *What the hell?* and headed, instead, for Bacchus' Lair. Parking was once more something of a problem, signifying the return to normal for the bars along Arnwood, and I had a strange feeling in the pit of my stomach when I realized that the nearest parking spot I could find on Arnwood was directly across from a now vacant lot that had been the former location of the Dog Collar.

The first show had just ended when I passed the security guard and climbed the stairs to Bacchus' Lair. The place was back to it's usual state of being packed, though a few tables were emptied by guys who wouldn't be staying for the second show. I looked around for Bob, and, not seeing him, decided to sit at the bar. I saw T/T working the crowd, and after a minute or so he made his way to the bar.

"Chile!" T/T boomed when he spotted me. "If it isn't my very favorite big ol' Dick!" That got a couple intense glances from others at the bar and, as usual, I was embarrassed as all hell to be singled out.

"Hi, Teddy," I said. "Buy you a drink?"

"Silly question!" T/T said, raising an arm to attract the bartender's attention and causing a clatter as the 30 or so bracelets he was wearing shifted from wrist to elbow. "What'cha doin' here all alone, darlin'?" he asked. "If you come lookin' for me, I'm all yours!"

The bartender brought T/T's double scotch, which he belted back in one toss. "Thanks, darlin'" he said. "You are here with someone, aren't you?"

"I'm supposed to meet Bob Allen," I said, "but I don't see him yet."

T/T looked around the room, as if confirming that Bob indeed was not there. "Well let's get you a table up close. When Bob comes in, he'll see you. 'Sides, you stay here at the bar and someone's goin' to try to put the make on you!"

Please, God, I thought.

Grabbing my drink before I had a chance to object, T/T led me to one of the empty tables at the foot of the stage. It was not near an exit, but I didn't want to make an issue of it. T/T put my drink down and made sure I was seated. "Now you enjoy the show, hear?" And with that, he disappeared down the hall toward the bathrooms.

While I've never been one of those people who won't go anywhere unless they have someone to go with, or wouldn't dream of eating in a restaurant alone, sitting by myself at a table in a gay bar surrounded by couples and groups did make me just a little self-conscious. Odd, when Chris and I were together and we'd see someone sitting by himself, we'd kind of feel sorry for him. Now the shoe was on the other foot.

Bob had not shown up by the time the house lights dimmed for the second show, so I just decided to sit back and enjoy it. Pretty much a carbon copy of the other times I'd seen the show, but still enough fun to make it worthwhile. And T/T was as outrageous as ever. He did a version of Sophie Tucker's "You Gotta See Momma Every Night" that brought down the house.

There was a new kid who did a pretty good Marlene Dietrich's "Falling in Love Again" and a campy version of "Lili Marlene".

And then it was time for Judy. If her selections had been a little on the more reflexive side the past few times I'd seen her, tonight she was on an upswing. She opened with "The Atchison, Topeka, and the Santa Fe", followed by "Get Happy," and ended with "Swanee." And this time, there was no doubt, she looked directly at me at least three times—quickly, but no mistaking the eye contact.

The audience, as usual, went wild and wouldn't let her off the stage. Finally, she relented for only the second time since I'd started coming to see her. She sat on the edge of the stage, directly in front of me. The lights dimmed to a single light-pink spotlight on her face, and she sang "Somewhere Over the Rainbow." And she sang it directly to me!

At the end of the song, the spotlight went out, and I could see—only because I was so close—her get up and disappear behind the curtain. Despite nearly five minutes of wild applause and whistles and calls of "Ju-dy! Ju-dy!" the curtains remained closed. The other performers came out for their curtain calls, and the show was over.

I was sitting there, finishing my drink and wondering what in hell *that* had been all about—she rarely had even seemed aware of the audience, let alone played so directly to just one guy in it—when the waiter came over and handed me a note. Puzzled, I opened it to read: *Come backstage.*

Thinking it was from T/T and not sure whether I wanted to go backstage or not, I hesitated a minute before deciding, again: *What the hell?* I flagged down the waiter who had brought me the note and asked him how I could get back to find T/T. He looked at me oddly: "It's not Tondelaya," he said. "It's Judy." And he pointed me to the hallway leading to the bathroom.

Okay, Hardesty, I thought as I started toward the hall. *What in the hell is going on here?* If, by some totally-out-of-left-field chance Judy had decided to make a pass at me, I really didn't dig drag queens. I vastly prefer men who aren't pretending to be…well…women. Still, my curiosity was pushing me into the hallway, and I knew I'd have to find out one way or the other.

I'd never really noticed before, but while the bathroom doors were at the end of the hallway on the left, there was also a doorway on the right, and I realized it was directly behind the stage. I should have knocked, but I opened it to find another short hallway paralleling the rear of the stage. At the end was an open door and I could see several of the drag queens removing their makeup, changing clothes, and talking and laughing among themselves. About halfway down, on the left, was a single closed door with a large gold star on it.

Okay, Hardesty. You're here! Do it! Taking a deep breath, I knocked.

"Come in." *Oh, Jesus! I knew that voice!*

I entered the room to see a seated form in a man's bathrobe, his back to me in the process of removing his contact lenses. A wig I recognized as the one Judy wore for the show was on a small stand on the dressing counter. I also recognized the sandy blond hair of the man in front of me, and I had a knot the size of a grapefruit in my stomach.

Putting the contacts carefully in their case, he got up and turned toward me for the first time.

Kevin!

He smiled, moving toward me and extending his hand.

"Hi," he said. "I'm Patrick."

CHAPTER 16

I somehow managed to take his hand and, despite my shock, was aware of its strength.

He stood there staring into my eyes and smiling. And still holding my hand.

"That's why we're called *identical* twins," he said, my confusion apparently being written all over my face. "I understand you've been looking for me."

"Well...uh...yeah," I managed to stammer.

"Kev was right," he said, pulling his head back slightly and looking me over slowly from head to toe like a rancher contemplating a prize bull.

"About what?" I managed to say, wondering when he was going to let go of my hand.

"You *are* sexy. How about a nice, hot fuck?"

Whoa, cowboys! Break time!

I managed to release my grip and back away a step or two. "Thanks for the offer," I said, "but I just screwed the waiter and two busboys on the way in here."

He laughed and shook his head. "I knew I liked you!" he said. "You've got balls—big ones, I'd guess—not like that little woosie brother of mine."

Part of me suspected I was way out of my league here, but the rest of me knew I had no idea what league that might be at the moment. "Yeah, well," I said, running my hand quickly over my chin, "I really did want to talk to you."

"About Kevin?"

"Well, yes, about Kevin. And about..."

"He's got the hots for you, you know," Patrick said, turning around to remove his robe and hang it on a clothes hook. He had his shorts on, but I could imagine what lay inside—hell, I'd seen it, on Kevin.

"What in hell gives you that idea?" I asked.

He turned toward me briefly to give me a big, sexy grin. "We *are* brothers, you know," he said, picking up a towel to wipe the remainder of his makeup off. "That 'I'm married so I can't be a queer' bullshit might work for dear old dad, but it don't mean squat to me. But why don't you hold on a second while I change, and we can go someplace and talk—like your place."

Jesus, the guy had balls, I had to admit. And while my head told me bringing Patrick to my apartment was not a good idea, my crotch was telling quite a different story.

I waited in silence while Patrick quickly dressed, then went to the door. I started to follow, but he shook his head and turned the deadbolt to lock the door from the inside. Then he motioned me toward the closet in one corner of the room. Puzzled, I followed as he swept the hangers—mostly Judy costumes but a few sets of men's shirts and pants—to either side to expose another door behind them. Opening it, he made an elaborate "after you" gesture with one hand and, when I stepped into a narrow stairwell leading down, he moved the clothes back into position, closed the door, and followed me down the stairs. The door at the bottom opened onto the alley behind Bacchus' Lair. *That's why no one ever saw Judy coming or going,* I thought!

"Which way's your car?" Patrick asked, and I motioned down the alley to the left.

"Well, let's go around the block this way," he said, heading to the right. "The street's closer here."

As we walked down the darkened alley, I could hear music coming from the second floor of one of the buildings on the other side of the alley. A piano. Beethoven. And suddenly I realized that we were passing directly behind Salvation's Door; both buildings backed up to the same alley!

Patrick glanced up toward the sound of the music and obviously read my mind. "Ironic, isn't it?" he said. "So close and yet so far apart. Little brother at his prayers and meditation," he said. "You and me going for one of the hottest fucks *you'll* ever have."

I was more than a little irritated by his last sentence. He was pretty damned arrogant to think that's what was going to happen. I was also pretty sure he was right.

*   *   *

Now here's a guy you met all of half an hour ago, I thought as we rode in relative silence to my apartment. *A guy who very well may be a total loon capable of just about anything, and you're primary concern at the moment is to get him into bed! Just how fucking stupid can you be?*

Well, anybody who is out to keep Chief Rourke from becoming governor can't be all bad, I rationalized—not very convincingly.

"Look, Patrick," I said, "I think maybe we should talk first ab…"

Patrick looked at me. "Fuck first. Talk later," he said.

Damn, I hated myself, but my crotch told me he was right.

Part of me was thinking *Jeez, Hardesty, you're a real slut!,* but I hastened to my own defense by reminding myself that I'd just come out of a monogamous (on my part) relationship of five years and was kind of out of practice on the etiquette of hard-core cruising. True, I'd had sort-of sex with Kevin, but that really didn't involve cruising. And if Patrick was anywhere near as good as his brother… Suffice it to say the Scorpio sex drive won out over Scorpio deductive reasoning, and it was as exciting as all hell.

*   *   *

We hadn't even closed the apartment door before Patrick started ripping—and I do mean ripping—my shirt off. We were all over one another, stumbling across the room and finally falling backward onto the sofa, then onto the floor. Patrick on top, then me, then Patrick, stripping clothes as we went, mouths locked together. Moaning, humping, groaning. We didn't even try to make it to the bedroom. Somehow we found ourselves in a wild head-to-foot, until Patrick broke away, flipped around so we were face to face again, and rolled me over on top. He wrapped his legs around my waist and reached down to guide me home....

Needless to say, I did things with Patrick that night that I had never known two human beings could do to/with one another. He had been absolutely right, it *was* one of the greatest nights of my life.

I woke up at 10:30 Sunday morning, in bed. Alone.

The apartment was a total shambles. We had done it in every single room in the place, including the kitchen and the bathroom. I was sticky from my chin to my thighs and desperately needed a shower (we'd been there, too, at one point). How I had the energy to stand up amazed me.

But Patrick had lied. He had said "Fuck first. Talk later." And we hadn't talked. Not in words.

And of course I had absolutely no idea of how to get in touch with Patrick. No phone number. No address. Just Bacchus' Lair, and they didn't have a show on Sunday nights. Which got me to thinking, Patrick Rourke might be a drag queen, but oh, my, strip him down to the basics, and....

I stood in the shower and had one of my little Hardesty-to-Hardesty talks. *Okay, Hardesty, now what's happening? Now you're falling for Kevin Rourke and Patrick Rourke?*

Who said anything about falling for anyone? Getting a trifle obsessed with, perhaps, but 'falling for?' Get a fucking life!

I was hoping against hope that Kevin would not call. What would I/could I possibly say to him? I sure as hell couldn't tell him I'd met his brother and fucked the stuffing out of him without finding out one single thing of the millions of things I wanted to find out. And I am one of the world's absolute worst liars.

But Kevin couldn't possibly know his brother was working

as a drag queen less than 200 feet from Salvation's Door, and I couldn't bring myself to tell him. Damn it, I had to nail Patrick down...*uh huh*...and get some answers.

Bob called just after I got out of the shower, to ask if we'd gone to Bacchus' Lair. When I told him that I had, he apologized and said he'd gotten involved with some friends and ended up playing cards all night. He asked how the show had been, and I told him 'fine.'

I just took it easy most of the day, not really in the mood to do much of anything except reflect on the night before and wonder for the 2,000[th] time what was going on between the two brothers and me.

Bacchus' Lair did not open until 6 p.m. on Sundays, and featured only a pianist as entertainment. I wrote a note with my phone number and the message "Call me!" addressed to "Judy" and gave the waiter $5 to let me slide it under her dressing room door.

*   *   *

C.C. informed me Monday that I would be accompanying the chief and the adult members of the Rourke clan on a four-day campaign swing of the state, beginning Tuesday. The primaries were almost here, and recent polls had shown the chief trailing slightly behind Senator Evans. McNearny had proposed the modern-day equivalent of a whistle-stop tour, concentrating on the smaller rural communities where closet conservatives were thought to dwell in great number. The chief, his family and his advisors would be traveling by chartered bus. I and Jim DeCarlo, another of C.C.'s staffers normally in charge of the Xerox room, would travel ahead of the bus in a rental van with banners, posters, press kits, bumper stickers, and assorted P.R. paraphernalia. Arriving 2 hours ahead of the bus, it was our duty to meet with the chief's local supporters and be sure they had all the materials they needed for a rousing spontaneous display of enthusiasm when the chief himself rolled into town. Having thus dispersed our materials, we would speed on down the road to the next stop and repeat the process.

I'd never spent much time in the rural part of the state, but was quickly reminded that my world—the world of gay bars, Sunday brunch, and Gay Pride rallies—was not the same world as the Bubba-land I found myself in, where pickup trucks outnumbered other vehicles by 200 to one, and where patriotism as the locals saw it went considerably beyond singing "God Bless America" on the 4th of July. For me, the whole experience was summed up in a gun-rack-in-the-rear-window pickup we were lucky enough to be stuck behind for about 30 miles on a two-lane road. It was covered with bumper stickers: "America for the Americans!" "America First!" "Buy American!" It was a Toyota.

Actually, the tour was a pretty shrewd political ploy. At each stop, Kevin would introduce the family, give a brief speech praising his father's accomplishments and plans for the future of the state, and then introduce the chief, who would recite one of five brief canned speeches prepared by his team and designed to fit the perceived particular interests of the community. If time allowed, and it usually didn't, the chief would take two or three questions from strategically placed supporters in the crowd. Again, everything was finely honed to avoid any possibility of spontaneity.

It also meant, of course, that I would have almost no opportunity to talk with Kevin and could not possibly hear from Patrick. Even the overnight stops were set up so that the van would stay wherever the bus's first stop would be in the morning.

That I had to share a room each night with Joe was bad enough; I didn't even have the freedom to go out alone to check out the wholesome, corn-fed hunks who somehow seem to abound in small-town America. Most of them were already married with two kids by the time they were 18, of course, but there were more than enough fleeting eye-contacts to make it pretty clear that one or two of them would be more than willing to see what they were missing.

*   *   *

The tour went relatively smoothly—the chief didn't stick his foot in his mouth more than a couple of times; Mrs. Rourke's task was to stand beside her husband and beam with pride (those who had never seen Kathleen Rourke beam with pride have missed a classic example of the actor's art). Sue-Lynn and Sean were on prominent display as often as possible; when Kevin was not speaking, he could be photographed with his arm (left arm, remember?) lovingly around Sue-Lynn's shoulder.

I took great pride on making it through the entire four days without yielding to the often overwhelming temptation to throttle Jim DeCarlo who insisted on outlining in excruciating detail every sexual encounter he had ever had from the age of fifteen to the present. I wouldn't have been interested even if Jim had been gay, but he was a card carrying Breeder and damn proud of it. By the time we got back into town on Friday afternoon, I swore that if I had to listen to one more glowing description of aroused female genitalia, I was going to stub out my cigarette in the guy's eyeball.

*   *   *

There were several messages on my machine, none of them from Patrick. I remembered then that Bacchus' Lair only did their full drag shows on Friday and Saturday nights. I wondered where Patrick was the rest of the time—if he was as promiscuous as Kevin said, it was a pretty sure bet he'd be known in some of the bars or baths around town. But there were a lot of bars. And quite a few baths.

The last thing I wanted to do was to go out after being on the road all week, but I felt I had really screwed up (again, no pun) by letting my crotch rule my head with Patrick. I also felt guilty for the feeling that I had somehow let Kevin, and myself, down, and I determined to make it right.

I called Bob, ostensibly to see how things were going with

him, but also to check to see if he might be at Bacchus' Lair—if he were, I couldn't risk trying to contact Patrick. It would open the door to too many questions. Luckily, Bob said he was staying in for the evening.

I debated on whether to take a nap after dinner and before getting ready to head to Bacchus' Lair for the second show—which of course triggered one of my little internal dialogues.

Getting set for another all night session, Hardesty?

No, damn it. I'm just tired. I'm not planning on any sex tonight.

Of course you aren't. And pigs can fly.

To prove myself wrong, I forced myself to stay awake and spent the evening chain smoking and watching TV.

*   *   *

I'd called ahead for a table near an exit, and arrived about ten minutes before the start of the second show. No sign of T/T, and I was mildly curious as to whether anyone had seen me going into Judy's dressing room. Of course whether they had or hadn't, I was willing to take bets that the waiter would have told everyone, especially given Judy's reclusive reputation.

I don't remember much of the show at all. Even T/T's set was something of a blur. Partly my being tired, I guess, and partly my continuing mind-vs.-crotch battle over the prospect of another meeting with Patrick. Well, this time I wasn't going to be so easily suckered. I had a goal that didn't involve my crotch, and I damned well was going to reach it.

When the house lights went out signaling the start of Judy's set, I had an odd knot in my stomach. She began with "I'm Nobody's Baby," followed by "Just in Time," and ending with "Zing Went the Strings of My Heart." She seemed to be studiously avoiding any direct eye contact, though I knew she was aware I was there. Apparently the word of my admission into the sanctum sanctorum had made her leery of being too obvious for the other employees. However, at the end of her last

number, she did give me a quick glance and an almost impercepti-
ble movement of her head indicating I was to come backstage
after the show.

Even before the applause died away, I was off in my own
little world, pondering the whole Judy/Patrick thing. When
Patrick was up there on stage as Judy, there was no question
in my mind that the correct word was "she." Patrick, at that
moment, *was* Judy Garland. But the minute the dress, wig, and
makeup came off, it was "he" without a doubt in the world. And,
oddly, Patrick as Judy left me physically cold, whereas Patrick
as Patrick....

My mind cut me off: *Yeah, yeah, yeah; enough philosophy
already!*

I took my time finishing my drink, and then got up and
headed for the hall to the bathroom and the dressing rooms. A
guy was buying a pack of cigarettes from the machine, so I waited
until he had finished and walked past me back into the main
room before stepping inside the door. To my surprise, T/T was
standing just inside, waiting for me. This was not the bubbly
Tondelaya O'Tool, or even T/T, but Teddy, and a very serious
Teddy at that. He took my arm and bent his head closer to mine,
and said in a low voice: "You be *very careful*, you hear?" Then
he turned without another word and headed back to join the
other performers in the main dressing room.

I knocked on Judy's dressing room door and once again heard
the familiar "Come in." Patrick was just removing the last of
his makeup, and looked up at me via the mirror.

"I got your message," he said, using a tissue wrapped around
the tip of his middle finger to remove a bit of eyeliner. "I called,
but you'd apparently already left the apartment. When I didn't
get you, I thought you'd probably show up here. You want a
quickie here first, or wait till we get to your place?"

He's doing it again, I thought, mildly pissed by his
automatic assumptions but weakening.

"We have to talk, Patrick," I said. "Talk first, fuck later."
That last part was added by my crotch; it wasn't what I'd

intended to say at all.

Patrick got up from his chair and reached for a shirt on the clothes rack. Without looking at me, he shrugged and said: "Whatever."

When he'd finished dressing, we did the locking-the-door-exit-through-the-closet routine and ended up in the alley again. As we walked past the back of Salvation's Door, we could hear the sound of a piano coming from the direction of Kevin's office. Liszt, this time. Patrick looked up toward the music.

"He's pretty good, isn't he?" Patrick said.

"Yes, he is," I said, and was surprised, in the dim light of the alley, to see an almost sad look on Patrick's face.

"Kevin plays. I sing," he said, almost to himself. And then his face changed again, and he was his old cocky self. "Let's move it along, hot stuff," he said. "I can't wait for another 12-inch injection of old Dr. Hardesty's Mad Root!"

Flattery will get you anywhere! I thought.

When we were safely in the car and I was pulling away from the curb, I decided that now was as good a time as any to start our long-overdue talk.

"How come you disappeared the other night?" I began.

"Glad you missed me!" Patrick said with a grin. "But honey, you better know right now I don't do sleep-overs. Too much like commitment, and I'm not big on commitment."

Point made, I thought.

"Why drag?" I asked.

"Why not?" he responded. "Look, I haven't the slightest doubt about whether I really want to have a dick or not. I find it's the guys who aren't so sure who have the problem with drag."

"Have you always done it?" I asked as we waited for a traffic light to turn green.

"Oh, sure, honey! All my life!" His voice had a sharpness and bitterness that startled me. He must have noticed my reaction, and his voice returned to is normal tone. "When Kevin and I were 8 years old, we were left home alone one day while dear old dad went to visit mother in the hospital—she'd just had Colleen. We were playing around the house, and went in to our parents' room—which was our first big mistake, since that room was strictly forbidden without knocking first and getting permission."

I got the feeling that Patrick was talking more to himself than to me. He apparently suddenly realized it, and shot me a quick sidelong glance before continuing.

"Anyway, we went into their closet and decided it would be fun to dress up like mommy and daddy. Kevin got dressed up as Daddy, and I put on one of mother's housecoats and a big picture hat." He paused and, without turning to look at him directly, I could see out of the corner of my eye an almost pained expression on his face. He was quiet a moment, then sighed and continued.

"So guess who chooses that very minute to walk into the room?" His voice was bitter. "Dear old Dad, of course, who proceeded to grab me by the shoulders, pick me up off the floor, and slam me into the wall so hard it knocked pictures off the wall in the other room, Then, just in case I didn't get his message, he proceeded to beat the crap out of me. Chipped a tooth, almost broke my arm. And I'm eight years old, for Christ's sake!"

I felt mildly sick to my stomach, and my loathing for the chief boiled dangerously close to the surface. I'd never understood before why he was nicknamed "The Butcher," but hearing what he'd done to his own children... I didn't know what to say.

"And Kevin?" I asked, finally.

Patrick laughed, but there wasn't even a hint of humor in it. "Kevin? Kevin was dressed up as Daddy, you see, so he was the little man. *He* was just playing a harmless child's game: dear old dad didn't even give him a second thought. But *me*....And my darling little brother just stood there while my father beat the shit out of me and he didn't do a God-damned thing! He..." His voice had begun to tremble, and he suddenly stopped talking and stared out the window.

You really want to know all this, Hardesty? I asked myself. And the reluctant answer was: *Yes.*

"And your working at Bacchus' Lair is way of getting back at your father?" I asked.

Patrick looked at me and shook his head. "Oh, no...I don't work at Bacchus' Lair. I own it. Grandpa Corchoran, who built up a tidy fortune in graft as chief of police, left Kevin and me a trust fund, not to be touched until we turned 25. The other kids weren't born yet. So when we reached 25, I took my money out and bought the bar. Did you know daddy owns the building—well, his corporation does. I thought it marvelous that while daddy hates fags, he has nothing against taking their money. And my doing drag there is just...well, sort of poetic justice."

*   *   *

When we entered my apartment this time, Patrick was considerably more subdued, as was I. I think he realized it was time he got everything out in the open. We sat in the two chairs flanking the fireplace, and I didn't even offer him a drink or coffee. I think we both were too preoccupied to notice, or to care.

"How old were you when you knew you were gay?" I asked.

Patrick shrugged. "Always," he said. "Our parents were such total shits—I can't recall one single time in my life when I saw my father kiss my mother. And if they weren't able to show affection for each other, you can be damned sure they couldn't show any for us. So we clung to each other—at first mostly figuratively, but more and more it became literally, too. After the little 'How-I-Began-My-Life-in-Drag' episode, they moved me out of our room and into a little guest room in the attic. But late at night, one of us would come to the other's room and we would just lay in bed and hold each other When we reached puberty, the holding got a little beyond holding and then a lot beyond holding. But we could never, ever sleep together!"

I was so absorbed in listening to Patrick's story, it never

occurred to me to interrupt him, and he didn't seem to notice.

"I recognized what we were right from the beginning. But not Kevin! Oh, no! Kevin got religion. We would finish a wild 69 that drove both of us crazy and Kevin would run into the bathroom to wash his mouth out and then he'd come back and rant and rave about what terrible, evil, perverted creatures we were, and how we were doomed to hell forever. That wouldn't stop him the next time he got a hard-on, of course, but it was always the same afterwards, and it got worse. Finally he wouldn't let me touch him—he'd go on and on about abominations and evil and the devil and how *he* had been saved from damnation because he had accepted Jesus Christ as his personal savior, and on and on and on.

"And the more he came under daddy dear's control and never questioned and never ever stood up for himself or for me, the more I went in the opposite direction. I rubbed their noses in it every chance I got. Daddy had his angel in Kevin; I made damn sure he got the Devil in me."

Finally I decided to say something.

"So you agreed to go away." I said.

"Yes. And it was the best thing I could ever have done. I found out I could be happy for the first time in my life."

"But you came back," I noted.

"Do you think I could have stayed away?" Patrick said. "And let dear old dad do to the entire state what he did to Kevin and me? Oh, no! Somebody has to stop him."

Finally! I thought. "And just how do you plan to do that?" I asked.

Patrick gave me a very wry smile. "I have my ways."

"But..." I started to say, but Patrick cut me off with a shake of his head.

Realizing he was not about to tell me and not wanting to push too hard, I opted for another track: "Will you at least see Kevin?" I asked.

Patrick looked at me as though I had surprised him somehow. "Do you really think I should?" he asked

"Don't *you* think so?" I asked.

"Kevin isn't ready," he said. "He can't face me. Kevin puts on a pretty white-bread face, but there's so much more going on in there you can't even begin to imagine! I will talk to him, though. There are a few things we have to say to one another."

Patrick leaned forward in his chair, put his elbows on his knees with his hands clasped in front of him, much as Kevin did. He looked at me soberly for a moment, then his face broke into a slow, wicked grin.

"*Now* can we fuck?" he asked.

We could.

CHAPTER 17

Patrick woke me around five by kissing me hard and slipping his tongue into my mouth. Despite our having been at it nonstop for over three hours, I was instantly ready to go again, but Patrick pushed me away.

"Gotta go," he said, getting out of bed to put his clothes on.

I started to get up to drive him...where? But Patrick pushed me back onto the pillow. "I called a cab," he said.

"Will you leave me your phone number?" I asked.

He had his back to me, putting on his pants, but I saw him shake his head. "No," he said. "I'll see you at the bar."

"But you will talk to Kevin?" I asked. "And try not to upset him this time?"

He turned to look at me, buttoning his shirt. "You've really got the hots for Kevin, haven't you?"

I shook my head. "It's not a matter of the hots," I said; "I'd just like to see the two of you make peace with one another."

Patrick looked at me rather strangely and once again a look of sadness crossed his face. "It's a little late for that now, I'm afraid."

"It's never too late," I said.

Patrick shrugged, blew me a kiss, and left.

The thought occurred to me that I should get up and follow him. I still had no idea where he lived or how I could reach him outside Bacchus' Lair. But I was just too damned tired to move, so I didn't.

*   *   *

C.C., on Monday, was almost giddy with smugness and self-importance. The polls in the wake of the chief's bus tour—which of course, as C.C. broadcast throughout the office, had been his idea from the beginning, but for which he magnanimously let McNearny take the credit—showed the chief had pulled substantially ahead of Senator Evans. This was hardly surprising, since the senator's campaign coffers were nowhere near as big as the chief's, and the primaries, now only two weeks away, were almost sure to give the chief the victory. The chief was so confident of winning that he had even considered submitting his resignation to the Police Commission prior to the outcome of the primaries, but cooler heads on his team prevailed. I rather wished they hadn't, since if he stepped down as chief and was then blown out of the water by whatever Patrick had in mind, he'd be neither governor *nor* police chief. The best of all possible worlds.

Kevin's speaking schedule continued unabated, and he was out of town with Sue-Lynn and Sean both Monday and Tuesday. I hoped Patrick would keep his word and not just call Kevin but keep from baiting him even further. I agreed with Patrick's assessment that there was a lot more going on inside Kevin than met the eye, and I was concerned that the incredible pressure he was under from all sides might crack him.

When Wednesday passed with no word from Kevin I was beginning to become concerned. It occurred to me Wednesday night when I got home from work that I'd not heard from either Tom or Don since our dinner at Rasputin's. I'd considered calling them earlier, but decided that could be interpreted as prying, so I held off. However, in an effort to take my mind off the Rourkes, I decided to call Tom, to check in for any new information on the fires— which seemed to have pretty much reached a standstill on all fronts.

I waited until after dinner before dialing Tom's number. He answered on the first ring.

"Hi, Tom," I said, and there was a brief pause before Tom responded.

"Dick?" he asked. "Oh, hi. When the phone rang I thought it might be Don."

"Aha!" I said. "Are you two becoming an item?"

A momentary pause and then a rather sheepish "Yeah. I guess you could say that. I'm really sorry we haven't talked to you since we all had dinner that night, but I guess we've been kind of…busy. I can't tell you how grateful I am, Dick…and how grateful Don is, too, I'm sure…for your having introduced us. He's fantastic! And he seems to like me, too."

"Well don't act so surprised," I said, genuinely pleased for both of them. "I really hope it works out for the two of you—you'll make a great couple."

"Yeah," Tom said again. "Don wasn't too sure at first whether he wanted to get into anything serious so soon after having lost his ex. But we've spent just about every night together since we met, and we haven't gotten tired of one another yet."

"Well, I probably should let you go if you're waiting for his call. Are you supposed to meet him later?"

"Not tonight," Tom said. "He was called out of town yesterday to help identify some remains they found up north somewhere. They needed a forensics expert rather than just the local medical examiner. Hopefully he won't be gone too long."

"Well, again, I'm really glad for you. But don't go forgetting your other friends just because you found each other."

"We won't," he said. "As a matter of fact, we'll probably be having a party before too long, and you're for sure invited!"

"Thanks," I said. "Oh, and before I forget, any news on the fires?"

"Afraid not. If we could find out who stole that file from the chief's office, we'd be one hell of a lot closer than we are. But all of a sudden, the lines of communication between the fire and police departments seem to have broken down. I think the police are really pretty unhappy with the realization that not only was someone able to steal something right out of the chief's office, but that it very well may have been one of their own. Whatever investigating they're doing, they're keeping it pretty much to themselves."

At that point, my doorbell rang, and I excused myself, telling Tom I'd give him a call in a couple of days.

I hadn't ordered a pizza and wasn't expecting any visitors, so made sure I checked the little peephole in the door. It was Kevin. Or was it Patrick? God, I would *never* be able to tell them apart! But when I opened the door, I was pretty sure it was Kevin, even before I glanced down to see the wedding ring. The expression on his face left little doubt as to which one of the brothers it was.

"Kev!" I said. "What's going on?"

"Can I come in?" he asked, and I immediately stepped back to let him pass.

"Of course! What's wrong?" I needn't have asked, of course: I knew he'd spoken with Patrick.

We went into the living room, and Kevin sat on the edge of the sofa. I swung one of the fireplace chairs around to sit opposite him.

"You talked to Patrick," I said rather than asked.

Kevin searched my face, his brows knit in confusion. "Patrick says you're a…a homosexual. A deviant. A pervert. A *faggot*! He said that…that you and he…" *God damn it, Patrick!* I thought. Kevin was shaking his head in disbelief. Then he reached out and took my hand tightly. When he spoke, his voice had the pontificating tone of his father.

"Homosexuals burn in hell, Dick. Homosexuals are an abomination in the eyes of the Lord. They do not deserve to exist in God's world. They are condemned to eternal fire, Dick."

I felt as though someone had poured a bucket of ice water over my head. *Oh, God! Please don't let him be saying what I think he's saying! Please!*

Kevin's grip on my hand tightened. "But I know you are not a homosexual, Dick. I know that Patrick's infinite evil made him tell those disgusting lies about you. You're my friend, Dick. I know you would never take Patrick's side against me."

I somehow managed to free my hand. "That's okay, Kevin,:" I said. "I do want what is best for you; I know you know that.

Whatever else has happened between you and Patrick, you are brothers and I know you love one another."

Kevin shook his head decisively. "Do you know what Patrick does, Dick? He dresses up in women's clothes and parades himself in front of a bunch of perverts and degenerates. And do you know what else?" I just looked at him without daring to say anything. "He does it in a pervert's bar in a building that is owned by our father! And less than a block from Salvation's Door! How can he *do* that, Dick? How can he?"

Kevin's voice, and his face, softened. "Patrick is evil, Dick," he said softly. "He will destroy me."

And yet again, even while Kevin was scaring the shit out of me, I felt sorry for him. I could not, in a thousand years, imagine what Kevin and Patrick must have gone through to become the totally fucked up individuals they had become. And Kevin's references to gays burning in hell...no. My over-sensitivity. He was just using standard fundamentalist rhetoric. That's all. Kevin couldn't......

"Kev," I said, forcing myself back to the present, "you've been under more pressure than any ten guys could hope to bear—the campaign, Patrick showing up, the explosion at the shelter. You can't let it get to you. You've got to relax. No one can destroy you if you don't let them. Now, why don't you let me take you home, and you can get a good night's sleep."

Kevin shook his head. "I can't, Dick," he said. "Not right now, at least. I'm late for my prayers and meditation, and I very much need them tonight, I'll go back to the shelter, and then later I'll go home, I promise. And I'm sorry if I sound a little... irrational...at times. I'll be fine. Really. God does not give us a larger burden than we can bear."

He got up to leave.

"Can I drive you?" I asked.

Kevin shook his head. "No, I have my car. But thank you for being here for me, and thank you for being my friend."

He extended his hand and I shook it. "Good night, Kev," I said.

"Good night, Dick." And he left.

I stood staring at the door for a full minute after it closed, my stomach churning, my mind a Fourth of July fireworks display of thoughts and emotions. Kevin could not have been saying what I heard him say. I mean, he could not possibly have been implying….*Shit, Hardesty! Shit! How do you get into these things?* And, more importantly, how do I get myself out?

*   *   *

Not five minutes later, the phone rang. I moved to it, feeling as though I were walking through molasses up to my knees.

"Hello?" I heard myself say.

"Dick?"

"Kevin?" I said, recognizing the voice.

"No, not that sick bastard. It's Patrick. We've got to talk. It's serious, and you're not going to like it." Why did that not surprise me?

Have you ever had a really bad cold and been all doped up on medication and felt like you were standing outside yourself watching everything you did in slow motion? That's pretty much how I felt. And I *didn't* like it. Not one bit. But I knew that wasn't what Patrick was talking about.

"I'm sure I'm not, Patrick," I said. "What is it?"

"Not over the phone," he said. "Can I come over? I can be there in half an hour,"

"I guess," I said, still in something of a daze. "Kevin just left," I heard myself add.

"I figured as much from your voice. Are you okay?"

"I'm not sure," I said honestly.

"I'll be right over," he said and hung up, leaving me staring at the telephone like some idiot who has no idea what a telephone is.

It seemed as though I had barely put the receiver back on the cradle when there was a knock at the door. I opened it, and Patrick strode into the room, obviously distraught.

"It's Kevin," he said.

"Kevin?" I said. "But you just…"

"No, no. *I'm* Patrick—sorry, I keep forgetting nobody can tell us apart. What I was saying was that it's Kevin who…" he paused. "I think we'd better sit down."

I hadn't moved the fireplace chair back yet, so I motioned Patrick to it and I sat on the sofa.

"Kevin is…Dick, Kevin is very, very sick. Even I had no idea of just how sick. He desperately needs help and I'm here to beg you to help me get it for him."

I was staring at him, listening to his words, and not allowing myself to comprehend what he was telling me.

"What do you mean, Patrick?" I asked. But in my heart of hearts, I knew.

"Kevin set those fires, Dick. All of them. Kevin killed those men."

I was glad we were sitting down—I felt dizzy and desperately sick. My immediate reaction, when I managed to regain a little control of myself, was that Patrick was lying; that Kevin was right and that it was Patrick who was psychotic and that he would do or say anything to…to what?

"Why?" I heard myself ask. "Why would he do such a thing?"

"To get even with me for being gay. To get even with me for leaving him. To get even with himself."

"How do you know?" I managed to ask. "How can you be sure?"

Patrick looked terribly sad. "He told me. On the phone. He started screaming at me for being gay and for leaving him, and he said it was all my fault, and that all homosexuals deserved to die and…" he paused and started to cry "…oh, Jesus, Dick. You've got to help him! He's my brother and I love him! I didn't want to leave him! I didn't!"

I got off the sofa and knelt in front of him. "It'll be okay, Patrick," I said. "I promise."

He stopped crying and tried to smile. "You're a good friend,

Dick," he said, and for some reason I got a chill down my spine.

As I got up, Patrick did also. "I've got to go," he said.

"You could stay if you wanted," I said, and I wasn't implying sex.

Patrick smiled. "I know," he said. "But I do have to go."

"We'll talk later?" I said, and he nodded.

As I walked him to the door, the phone rang.

"You'd better get that," Patrick said. And with a wave, he left.

Something's happening! I told myself. *Something's happening!!*

I caught the phone on the third ring. "Hello?"

"Dick? It's Don. I have some news I think you might want to hear."

I knew what it was, but prayed I didn't.

"Go ahead," I said, and sat down on the edge of the sofa.

"I was called in on a forensics I.D. of a skull found by a couple kids on the riverbank about ten miles south of Neelyville. Dental records confirmed the identification, down to the chipped front tooth. It's Patrick Rourke."

CHAPTER 18

"It can't be," I heard somebody using my voice saying. "Patrick doesn't have a chipped front too..." *Oh, Jesus! Oh, Jesus! The beating the chief had given 8-year old Patrick while Kevin looked on and did nothing....*

"The department notified the family earlier this evening," he said. "They...."

"Thank you, Don," I heard myself say, and I hung up the phone without even saying goodbye.

And then I cried.

*   *   *

When I finally pulled myself together, I called Bob Allen, waking him up.

"Bob," I said, not apologizing for the lateness of the call, "we've got to talk. Now."

My tone of voice must have startled him, because all he said was: "I'll be right down."

*   *   *

I did not go to work Thursday morning, nor did I call. I'd personally hand C.C. my resignation the coming Monday.

Bob called an emergency meeting of the owners of the six burned out bars and officers of the Bar Guild for noon on Thursday at Bob's apartment. I told them everything, in detail, and then outlined the plan Bob and I had sat up until dawn working on. Had I been in less of a state of semi-stupor, the fact that there was very little dissension from the group would have both relieved and pleased me.

With the group still in the room, I called the chief's office to arrange an immediate appointment. I was informed that the chief was in seclusion at home with his family, and that appointments had to be made through proper channels and may or may not be approved depending on the nature of the proposed meeting, the chief's busy schedule, etc.. I then called the chief's home—I still had his unlisted number from our initial Sunday Supplement contact. To my total surprise, Kevin answered the phone.

"Rourke residence." He sounded very calm, very professional.

"Kev...it's Dick," I said. "I...I was just calling to see how you're doing."

"Thanks so much for calling, Dick. It's very kind of you." His voice lowered to a whisper. "Don't believe what you read in the papers, Dick. It's all a mistake. Patrick is alive."

Once again, I felt a tremendous wave of sadness. "I know he is, Kev," I said. "I just wanted to see how you were doing. Take care of yourself, and we'll talk later, okay?"

"Okay," he said. "And thanks again for calling. It's nice to know someone cares."

Shit! If I hadn't been in a room full of guys who couldn't be expected to understand, I'd have started crying again.

If I couldn't get to the chief directly, I'd try the next best thing. I called Charles McNearny's office and told his secretary it was urgent that I talk with him. There was a moment's pause, and then McNearny came on the line, sounding puzzled. "Dick," he said in his hale-fellows-well-met voice; "what a pleasant surprise. What can I do for you?"

"Please excuse me if I sound a bit melodramatic, Mr. McNearny, but it is urgent...and I stress the word 'urgent'... that I have a private meeting with the chief today."

There was a long pause, and then "I'm afraid that wouldn't be possible, Dick. The chief is with his family today; I don't know whether you've heard the..."

"I've heard," I interrupted, "and that is exactly why I must speak with the chief. I have information that he cannot ignore."

Another pause, and then a very suspicious: "That wouldn't be some sort of threat, would it, Dick?"

"Not a threat, Mr. McNearny, but a fact. And there is far more at stake here than the chief's political ambitions."

"Can you tell me what this is all about? I can pass it on to the chief."

"What I have to say to the chief you do not want to hear. Trust me."

"Well, Dick, as the chief's primary adviser, I'm afraid I would have to be present at any meeting with the chief…provided I can arrange one."

"If you insist," I said. "How soon can you get back to me?"

"Today?"

"Today. You have my number. I'll be waiting for your call."

"I'll see what I can do," McNearny said, and hung up.

Since everyone had been in the same room when I made the call, I had only to tell them McNearny's response. I suggested that since McNearny would want to be present for any meeting, that Bob should come with me as a representative of the Bar Guild, and they agreed that both Bob and I should represent them. They all wanted to be there, of course, but understood the impracticality of too many people present.

I thanked them all for their support and excused myself to return to my apartment and await McNearny's call.

*   *   *

Kevin Rourke had set the fires that wiped out seven businesses and caused the deaths of 29 innocent men, including Ramón. But there was not a jury in the civilized world which would convict him—and even if it would, what possible punishment could it mete out to equal the hell of his life? No, the person ultimately responsible for everything that had happened was Police Chief Terrence Rourke, and it was he who should pay. Even Bob had agreed, and helped me convince the

Bar Guild that more good could be gained from extracting some degree of justice from the chief than from prosecuting Kevin.

And as to Kevin himself: why did I have such strong feelings for him, and why couldn't I put those feelings into words? Sadness? Compassion? Sympathy? Empathy? I've never been able to bear seeing anything or anyone suffer, and Kevin was the most truly pathetic human being I personally had ever encountered. That he was so totally lost and alone was bad enough, but that he believed I was his friend....How could I not be? And in some indescribable way, I think I was. Patrick was not around to protect him; maybe I could.

I had not been in the apartment more than ten minutes when the phone rang. It was Charles McNearny, though he did not bother to identify himself. He merely said:

"Seven o'clock. My office" and hung up.

I didn't feel like going back up to Bob's apartment, so I just called and gave him the word, asking him to pass it on to any of the Guild members still there.

*   *   *

I didn't have my customary before-dinner drink. I didn't have dinner, either. While I wanted a stiff drink—or five—badly, I wanted more to be sure I had my full faculties when talking with the chief. And as for dinner, food was the last thing on my mind.

I kept thinking of Kevin and Patrick and wondering why in hell I hadn't caught on to it all a lot earlier. God knows there were enough clues. Kevin's "prayers and meditations" coincided with Judy's on-stage appearances. It would be easy enough to slip back and forth between the shelter and the back entrance to Bacchus' Lair. And the music Patrick and I heard—and yes, I still thought of Patrick as a separate person—had to have come from the tape recorder I'd seen on the piano in Kevin's office.

But what had triggered Kevin in the first place? He'd probably just been hanging on to his sanity by a thread for years—most definitely since Patrick's death—and the pressures just kept building. The timing of everything, the opening of Bacchus' Lair and the first of the bar fires, was undoubtedly linked to the chief's decision to run for governor. What was it Patrick had said? That he couldn't let his father do to the state what he had done to Patrick and Kevin?

And where did Kevin's elaborate tale about Patrick's disappearance come from—the chief's plan to send him off, the bank account in New York? I honestly think Kevin believed it. It was the only way he could avoid facing the unbearable reality that the only person whom he had ever truly loved, or truly loved him—that half of himself—was dead.

It would not have been difficult for Kevin, who had ready access to the chief's office—or could have seen them had the chief brought them home at any point—to take the report on Tamasini's arson records

The explosion at the fund raiser I was less sure of. I knew there were real problems with the oven. But it might have been Patrick's way of sending a message to his father. The explosion could have been much worse, but Sue-Lynn and Sean were in the dining room—in the far back of the room.

I'd never know on that one.

The sex at the S.A.P.C. meeting—was it Kevin, or Patrick? I suspected it may have been something of a crossover; Kevin had acted as though he was totally unaware of it the next morning, and he may not have been, but it may just have been Kevin's giving in to his own gayness.

And no matter how hard I tried not to think of it, my mind kept going back to Kevin's terrible loneliness, loss, and ambivalence toward his brother. I'd often heard and read of how the bond between identical twins could never be fully understood by those who are not in that position. Under the most ideal of conditions, that bond would be intense—given Patrick and Kevin's family, it was incomprehensible. Patrick had the guts Kevin never had; but for Kevin to sacrifice his own desires for the sake of his domineering parents took a sort of guts, too. And what must Patrick's disappearance have done to Kevin?

And lastly, Patrick. I truly, truly did not want to think of Patrick and how he had really died. If Kevin knew, which I doubted, he could never say; if the chief had indeed had a hand in it—also unthinkable—he certainly would never admit to it. I preferred to think that Patrick had died as everyone assumed he had—simply fallen into the river when the bluff broke away. But I knew in my heart of hearts that I would be dreaming, for many years, of that bluff by the river and what really happened there.

*   *   *

Neither Bob nor I spoke much on our drive to McNearny's office. I was mainly concerned that I not, when actually confronting the chief, give in to my barely-under-control rage against the chief—against "The Butcher." I told Bob to keep an eye on me, and to jump in if I started losing it.

We arrived at exactly two minutes to seven, and McNearny was waiting at the glass front door of the darkened building to let us in. Without a word, he led us to his office where the chief, in full uniform in an obvious move to intimidate us, sat in a leather chair beside McNearny's desk. He did not get up when we entered the room. There were no handshakes.

McNearny motioned Bob and me to two chairs facing the desk, then moved behind it to take his seat. When Bob and I were seated, McNearny leaned back in his chair and said:

"Now, exactly what is this all about?"

I took a deep breath, and began: "This," I said, nodding in Bob's direction, "is Bob Allen, owner of one of the seven gay bars burned in recent months." I noticed a look of contempt flash across the chief's face. I ignored it. "Bob's lover, Ramón, was one of the 29 men who died in the Dog Collar fire. Bob is also a member of the Bar Guild, and it is as spokesmen for that group that we are here."

The chief's look of contempt returned. "This is hardly the time or place..." he began, but I interrupted.

"No, Chief Rourke, this is precisely the time and the place."
I glanced briefly at McNearny. "What I am about to say is not
a threat. Nor is it an invitation to a discussion. It is a simple
statement of facts, and how you respond to it is up to you.

"The fact is that Kevin is responsible for all seven fires,
including the fire at the Dog Collar and it's resultant deaths."
McNearny looked totally incredulous. Interestingly, the chief's
expression did not change by so much as a flickered eyelash.

"You can't…" McNearny began, but I cut him off with a
raised hand.

"I can," I said. "I am ready to submit a report of everything
I know to the arson squad tomorrow morning. Whatever
concrete evidence we do not have, the arson squad can provide."
McNearny looked at the chief, who continued to stare directly
at me.

"Kevin started the fires, but the responsibility lies elsewhere," I said, returning the chief's stare. "In a way, Kevin is
as much a victim of the circumstances which led to the fires as
those who died in the Dog Collar. Bob, the other members of
the Bar Guild, and I agree on that point.

"Having said that, I will now outline our recommenda-
tions—which I assume you will see as more than recommenda-
tions: First, the chief will withdraw from the governor's race.
He has ample valid reasons to do so, under the circumstances."

McNearny started to speak, but it was the chief's hand, this
time, that stopped him.

"It is my understanding," I continued, "that the chief will
be eligible for early retirement at the end of next year. It is our
recommendation that he take it.

"Secondly," I continued, "Kevin is to receive immediate
psychiatric care in a facility able to deal nonjudgmentally with
his condition, though speaking strictly from the position of one
who has come to know and care for him, Kevin is shattered into
so many pieces I doubt he can ever be put back together again.

"Third. the official unofficial policy of this police department
in regards to the harassment of gay bars, gay establishments,

and the gay community at large will cease. If we are in violation of the law, we expect to be held accountable for it…but we are not to be singled out and targeted. We simply expect to be treated like everyone else,"

I was silent for a moment, and the chief said: "And in return for which…?"

I addressed myself directly to the chief. "In return for which a great many details of the chief's personal life will remain personal. Kevin—and Patrick—have suffered more than enough; we have no wish to cause what remains of the family any further pain."

I fell silent again. McNearny had been staring at the chief with a look of total incomprehension, but did not try to interrupt again. Finally, the chief pursed his lips and said: "Anything else?"

"No," I said. "That pretty much does it."

We all sat in silence for what seemed like an eternity, until the chief said: "You'll have our response within 48 hours."

"No," I said, shaking my head. "Kevin. Kevin first. Immediately."

The chief nodded.

"We will be keeping a close watch on Kevin's treatment—" I said, still staring directly at the chief, "—and you did understand what I was referring to when I used the word 'nonjudgmentally' in selecting a facility for his care?"

The chief nodded again.

I got up from my chair, followed by Bob, who gave me a puzzled look.

"Then we'll be leaving. Mr. McNearny, if you could unlock the door for us?"

McNearny got out of his chair, expressionless, and led us from the office to the front door, which he unlocked and pushed open for us.

Neither Bob nor I spoke until we got into the car.

"Was it just me, or was that too easy?" Bob asked.

"Not really," I said, waiting until a truck went by before

pulling out into traffic. "He really didn't have a choice. Either way, his political career is over and he knows it. The chief is a bigot, a bully, and a loathsome human being. But he is not stupid. I doubt he knew, or knows, everything. But he knows enough, and he's probably known all along that Kevin was in serious need of help, but just refused to face it. As long as Kevin was the good little breeder son he always wanted, he could probably overlook a lot. I'm still not sure he knows about 'Patrick,' and in a way I hope he doesn't. Patrick belongs to Kevin. He always has. I just hope that some day Patrick and Kevin can come to terms with one another, and realize that love doesn't end with death." I looked at Bob, and reached out to pat his leg. "As if I had to tell you," I said.

*   *   *

Chief Rourke withdrew from the race for governor the next day, citing family obligations relating to the discovery of his one son's remains and the subsequent emotional breakdown of his oldest surviving son. Kevin was never charged with any of the arsons or the deaths, and though his involvement was widespread knowledge, the exact details and circumstances were never made public. Everyone seemed satisfied that the issue was resolved.

I mailed my resignation to Carlton Carlson & Associates on Saturday and never looked back.

A month or so later, Bob, I, Tom, and Don got together for dinner at Rasputin's. I had apologized to Don for having hung up on him after he'd told me about Patrick, but he understood. He and Tom were planning on moving in together, and Tom was considering an offer from a large insurance company to serve as their arson investigator/ arbitrator.

Bob was busy preparing for the reopening of his bar, which he had decided would have a new name: Ramón's.

I'd given quite a bit of thought, in the intervening weeks, to exactly where I wanted to take my life, now that my halcyon days with old C.C. were over, and I'd made a decision. I had just been waiting for tonight to run it past my friends, hoping they'd agree it was a good idea, but intending to pursue it whether they did or didn't.

But before I had a chance to bring it up, the three of them exchanged glances, and Bob said: "We've got the perfect job for you. I was talking with some other members of the Bar Guild, and they agreed."

"What?" I said. "I should open a bar?"

"No," Tom said. "We all think you should seriously think about becoming a private investigator. I always told you you were a nosy bastard, and this way you could be nosy and get paid for it!"

Don nodded. "If it hadn't been for you, Chief Rourke might have been our next governor, and God only knows what would have happened with the fires."

"And I'm sure the Guild members would be able to keep you supplied with referrals," Bob added. "Will you think about it?"

I took yet another quick mental inventory of the current situation:

Chris was happy and well in New York.

Bacchus' Lair had closed.

T/T had moved to New Orleans to take a job at a world-famous drag club.

Salvation's Door closed, its flock being transferred to a new city-run shelter three blocks down on Boyle.

And construction had begun on a drive-through dry-cleaners on the site where the Dog Collar had stood.

The times, I thought, *they are a'changin'.*

I smiled at Don, Tom, and Bob in turn.

"Funny you should mention that," I began....

The End

YOUR PRIMARY SOURCE

for print books and e-books

Gay, Lesbian, Bisexual

on the Internet at

http://www.glbpubs.com

e-Book Fiction by such leading authors as:

Bill Lee	Chris Kent
Mike Newman	William Tarvin
Byrd Roberts	Veronica Cas
G-M Higney	Jim Brogan
Robert Peters	Veronica Cas
Kurt Kendal	Thomas R. McKague
Richard Dann	

and of course, Dorien Grey

Works available for downloads
(as low as $1 per short story)
in a wide variety of formats to
suit your particular taste and style